Alfred Moore Waddell

A Colonial Officer and His Times - 1754-1773

A Biographical Sketch of Gen. Hugh Waddell, North Carolina

Alfred Moore Waddell

A Colonial Officer and His Times - 1754-1773
A Biographical Sketch of Gen. Hugh Waddell, North Carolina

ISBN/EAN: 9783337155278

Printed in Europe, USA, Canada, Australia, Japan

Cover: Foto ©Raphael Reischuk / pixelio.de

More available books at **www.hansebooks.com**

A COLONIAL OFFICER AND HIS TIMES.

1754–1773.

A BIOGRAPHICAL SKETCH

OF

GEN. HUGH WADDELL,

OF

NORTH CAROLINA.

WITH NOTICES OF THE FRENCH AND INDIAN WAR IN THE
SOUTHERN COLONIES; THE RESISTANCE TO THE STAMP
ACT IN NORTH CAROLINA (WITH COPIES OF ORIGI-
NAL DOCUMENTS NEVER BEFORE PUBLISHED);
THE REGULATORS' WAR; AND AN HIS-
TORICAL SKETCH OF THE FORMER
TOWN OF BRUNSWICK, ON THE
CAPE FEAR RIVER.

BY
ALFRED MOORE WADDELL.

RALEIGH, N. C.
EDWARDS & BROUGHTON, Publishers.
1890.

TO THE MEMORY

OF

MY GOOD AND GIFTED FATHER, WHO BORE, WITH ADDED
HONORS, THE NAME

HUGH WADDELL,

THESE PAGES ARE REVERENTLY DEDICATED.

No. 59.

LORD HILLSBOROUGH:

NEWBERN, 28th January, 1771.

The death of Mr. Heron and Mr. Eustace McCulloh's resignation of his seat in Council, making two vacancies in his Majesty's Council of this Province, I take the liberty to recommend for the King's nomination the three* following gentlemen as properly qualified to sit at that Board, viz: Colonel Hugh Waddell, Mr. Marmaduke Jones, and Sir Nathaniel Dukinfield.

Colonel Waddell had the honor to see your Lordship about two years since in England. He honorably distinguished himself last war while he commanded the provincials of this Province against the Cherokee Indians, possesses an easy fortune, and is in much esteem as a gentleman of honor and spirit. * * *

---

*NOTE BY THE AUTHOR.—In all cases of vacancy in the Council, three names were forwarded from which a selection was made.

PREFACE.

To any one in possession of material, however small, which, if published, would prove to be of historical value, the exhortation of Carlyle, "Were it but the infinitessimalest fraction of a product, produce it," may well be addressed; and to none with more propriety than to a North Carolinian. The meagreness of the early public records of North Carolina, and the carelessness with which the history of the State has been written, have long been complained of by the historians of the United States, and have caused almost every notable and creditable event in that history to be doubted or denied. Nor has this neglect been remedied by biographical literature, for—excepting McRee's "Life and Correspondence of James Iredell," Caruthers's "Life of Caldwell," and Hubbard's "Life of General William R. Davie"—no volume aspiring to the title of a biography has ever been published of a North Carolinian, as such. The lives of some natives of the State—the three Presidents, Jackson, Polk and Johnson, for example—have been written, but these lives were passed out of the State, and were not identified with her history. We are almost as destitute of that sort of literature concerning our distinguished dead as we are of statues or monuments to their memory. The volumes of Colonial Records, recently obtained in England under an Act of the General Assembly, and now being published under the intelligent super-vision of Secretary of State Saunders, will supply the long-desired material, and will, doubtless, stimulate some student to the patri-otic task of writing a history which will be worthy of the State.

This little book, which is intended for North Carolina readers, and cannot be expected to have much circulation beyond the limits of the State, is accurate, if nothing else; and, while purporting to be merely a very imperfect biographical sketch of General Hugh Waddell, gives some information in regard to men and events in the Colony between the years 1754 and 1773 which is not familiar to most readers.

A sense of duty, stimulated by the expressions of regret in which several writers have indulged, that no sketch of General Waddell had ever appeared, prompted me to undertake it, notwithstanding the difficulties to be encountered.

There was ample material for his biography in his letters, papers, and official correspondence, which had been carefully preserved by his son, and which would have thrown light on the events occurring in the Province and elsewhere during the interesting period in which he lived, but the very means adopted to give value to this material resulted in a total loss of it. His son loaned it to Dr. Hugh Williamson, who had been a member of Congress before, at the time of, and subsequent to the adoption of the Federal Constitution, and who was then (about the year 1800) writing a history of North Carolina in New York; but although the most strenuous efforts were made to recover the papers after Dr. Williamson's

death in 1819, they could not be found, and all
trace of them was lost.   He not only failed to
preserve and return them, as he promised to
do, but made very little use of them in his two
queer and unsatisfactory volumes.

Dr. Williamson, although a man of culture
and integrity, was very careless and eccentric,
as his whole career proves, and while his history contains some facts not elsewhere to be
found, and is marked in some passages by
vigor and elegance of style, he betrays his
Keltic origin in the climax, and concludes his
work by a long, elaborate, and utterly irrele-
vant dissertation on fevers.

ALFRED MOORE WADDELL.

WILMINGTON, N. C.,
    January, 1889.

CONTENTS.

INTRODUCTORY.

The contest between European powers for
supremacy in America, which began with the
first settlements in the country, did not assume
serious proportions until towards the middle
of the eighteenth century, when the increasing
trade and population of the New World and the
vast possibilities which its future promised,
attracted the attention and excited the cupidity
of those powers. In the year 1755, the struggle between France and England, which,
because of the exhaustion of both parties, had
temporarily ceased with the Treaty of Peace
at Aix-la-Chapelle in 1748, was renewed by
France with increased vigor, not only in
Europe, but also in India and America. On
this continent she claimed the valleys of the
St. Lawrence and the Mississippi, and undertook to hem in all the English settlements by
a series of fortifications, and to deny to the
settlers the right to cross the Alleghany Moun-
tians. In pursuance of her purpose, after

securing the Northern frontier by a chain of
posts extending from Canada along the lakes
and rivers to the back of those settlements,
she had, as early as the month of January,
1753, seized an English truck-house in the
Twigtwees nation, and carried the traders as
prisoners to Canada; and in the latter part of
that year she built Fort Du Quesne on the
Ohio, and erected another fortification on the
headwaters of the Alabama river—meantime
practicing the shrewdest diplomacy in concili-
ating and making treaties with all the Indian
tribes from Canada to Louisiana.   A new life
seemed to be infused into the administration
of French interests at home and abroad, while
the condition of England was, for once in her
history, well-nigh pitiable.   Imbecility marked
her counsels, and disaster followed her arms.
After the miserable failure of Braddock's expedition against Fort Du Quesne in 1755, which
even the butchery in which it ended could
scarcely save from universal ridicule, and at
the close of the year, when the alliance between
England and Prussia was made, there were,
according to a reliable authority,* but three

---

*Newcastle's "preparations for the great struggle before
him may be guessed, from the fact that there were but three
regiments fit for service in England at the beginning of 1756.'·
Green's Short History, page 716.

regiments fit for service in England. The
following two years, the first of the Seven
Years' War—than which "no war has had
greater results on the history of the world, or
brought greater triumphs to England"—were
so freighted with disaster to her that universal
gloom and despondency prevailed. She was
humiliated by Admiral Byng's defeat by Admiral Galissoniere in the Mediterranean, by
the shameful retreat of the Duke of Cumberland with an army of fifty thousand men before
a French force on the Weser, and his agreement by the Convention of Closter-Seven to
disband his forces, and by similar events elsewhere, until "even the impassive Chesterfield,"
says the authority above quoted, cried in despair,
"We are no longer a nation."

It was at this critical period that the genius
of the greatest of English statesmen, William
Pitt, asserted itself, and immediately a series
of the most splendid triumphs in English history began. Frederick the Great said, "England has been a long time in labor, but she
has at last brought forth a man." Well might
he say it, for Pitt was his mainstay through
all his struggles, and the support he gave to

Prussia led to the creation of the German Empire of to-day, just as his breaking down of the barriers which the French sought to establish in America laid the foundation of the United States. In this way Pitt had, indeed, "unconsciously changed the history of the world."

Previous to this time the American Colonies, in the South especially, had suffered from Indian wars, from pirates, and from the Spaniards, who often threatened and sometimes attacked the coast towns.

For a century Spain had maintained a sickly show of authority in Florida, where she had erected one or two forts which were occupied by a small force, but had made no attempt at any further occupation of the territory, or development of its resources.

The jurisdiction over the West Indies was divided. France held Canada, Acadia (or Nova Scotia) and Louisiana. In the two first named the population was, in 1754, about seventy thousand, and in the latter territory about ten thousand. The English held the territory on the Atlantic seaboard from Canada to Georgia, and numbered at the same time about one million one hundred and sixty thousand.* They afterwards acquired Canada and Nova Scotia.

The governments in the English Colonies differed in name more than in character. Some were called Provincial, some Proprietary, and some Charter governments, but all were ultimately accountable to the Crown. These Colonies soon became very valuable as sources of revenue to Great Britain.

Before the middle of the century they were consuming about one-fifth of the woollen manufactures of the mother country—which constituted at that time her chief staple—and more than twice the value of these woollens in linen and calico, while the consumption of silk, furniture, trinkets, and East India goods was large. (In this connection it may be of interest to state that as early as 1716, according to a memorial of Mr. Beresford to the Commissioners of Trade and Plantations, silk culture had been tried in South Carolina, and the product had been sent to London where it was manufactured, "and proves to be of extraordinary substance and lustre.") They sent her valuable cargoes, especially of tobacco, which increased her shipping, gave employment to

*Montcalm and Wolfe, by Francis Parkman. Vol. I, page 20, (1885).

her people, and aided materially in keeping the balance of trade in her favor as against Holland, Portugal and Spain. Except as a barrier against the French in Canada, the acquisition of Nova Scotia was not a valuable one to England, as the products of that territory did not add to the resources of the latter, like those of the other Colonies.

Massachusetts did a larger and a more varied trade than any of them, and was the only Colony in which manufactures were carried on to any extent. The other Northern Colonies exported, principally, lumber, fish, live stock, and some naval stores, while the Southern Colonies shipped tobacco, rice, beef, pork, provisions, naval stores and lumber—the last named product going, as did the lumber and live stock of the Northern Colonies, chiefly to the West Indies. In Mr. Beresford's "Memorial," above alluded to, occurs the following: "There are also great quantities of cedar and cypress, far exceeding any Norway deals, being free from knots, of curious white color, great lengths, proper for flooring of the most magnificent buildings. The cedar for some uses far exceeds any other sort of wood, and, at the request of some noblemen and gentlemen of this nation, hath been brought into this kingdom, but the importers being obliged to *pay duty for it as sweet wood*, amounts to a prohibition." (The italics are not Mr. Beresford's.)

Outside of New England—where almost from the first settlement it had been enacted that "every township, after the Lord hath increased them to the number of fifty householders, shall appoint one to teach all children to write and read; and when any town shall increase to the number of a hundred families, they shall set up a grammar school"—there were very few schools in the country, even of the most elementary kind, and not a half dozen newspapers. The wealthier class sent their sons to England to be educated, while the poorer were either destitute of knowledge, or possessed only such as could be obtained at their own firesides. Agriculture, trade—which was largely in the form of barter—and fighting the Indians, occupied the attention of the people—of the Southern Colonies especially—almost exclusively.

In the Province of North Carolina the Proprietary Government, which was established in 1663, ended in 1728 when the Crown purchased the interest of seven of the eight Proprietors—Lord Carteret retaining his share—and on the 2d July, 1752, when Georgia was

2

surrendered by her Trustees to the King, there were only two Proprietary Governments left in the country, viz., Maryland and Pennsylvania, and some of the Royal Governors were anxious to see these surrendered.*

All the Southern Colonies were in a defenceless condition, both as to their Western frontiers and their sea-ports. The two Carolinas—which were *nominally* separated in September, 1720, when Sir Francis Nicholson was commissioned *royal* Governor of *South* Carolina, although no boundary line had then been even commenced between them—and the Province of Georgia were exposed to attacks from the French and Indians of the Mississippi river settlements, who, before 1735, had built what was called the Alabama fort in the Creek nation, and had fully garrisoned and mounted it with fourteen pieces of artillery, and later had attempted to build another fort nearer these English settlements.

The Creeks were quite numerous and were among the most formidable of the tribes of the South, as were also the Choctaws and Chickasaws. The Cherokees, Catawbas, and other tribes occupied the territory between them and

*Dinwiddie Papers. Vol. II, page 273.

the English settlements, and were not so war-like in disposition, although as cunning and merciless when roused.

In Florida the Spaniards had now several strong garrisons, the chief of which was St. Augustine, and they controlled the Indians of that territory.

While they claimed jurisdiction over a much larger area than was in their actual possession, they were not as active and enterprising in pushing their claims, and in making alliances with the Indians as the French, who, after the Mississippi Company surrendered their country to the French King, migrated from Canada in considerable numbers to the valley of that river, and acquired complete control of all the Indians in that region.

In 1741 an expedition was fitted out against the Spaniards at Carthagena, on the coast of New Grenada, near the Isthmus of Darien, to which North Carolina contributed a force, under Captain James Innes, but, after a siege which proved unsuccessful, the forces were re-embarked on Admiral Vernon's fleet and returned. In retaliation the Spaniards, several years after, made forays along the coast, attacking different places, and amongst others the town of Brunswick on the Cape Fear river, eighteen miles below Wilmington.

The population of these Provinces was sparse, and scattered chiefly along the coast belt, but notwithstanding the serious injury to their prosperity which external foes thus inflicted, and the additional embarrassments caused by the corrupt and inefficient government from which some of them suffered, there was a steady increase of population and trade.

In North Carolina, during the administration of Governor Gabriel Johnston, who, at the time of his death in 1752, had been Governor for eighteen years, the white population had increased more than three-fold, and at the date above mentioned had reached forty-five thousand. The exports for the year 1752 were three thousand and three hundred barrels of pork and beef, seven hundred and sixty-two thousand staves, sixty-one thousand five hundred and eighty bushels of corn, one hundred hogsheads of tobacco, sixty-one thousand five hundred and twenty-eight barrels of tar, twelve thousand and fifty-five barrels of pitch, ten thousand four hundred and twenty-nine barrels of turpentine, and thirty-thousand pounds of deer-skins, besides an unknown quantity of wheat, rice, potatoes, bacon, lard, indigo, tanned leather, lumber and other articles.*

---

*Martin. Vol. II, 59. See *post.*, Ch. VI, 217.

The currency, that perpetual source of trouble, had, during the same period, steadily risen towards its proper value.* Immigration had set in from Scotland, Ireland and Germany, and from Pennsylvania and Virginia; and these settlers had located themselves from the coast to that part of the country of the Cherokees and Catawbas east of the Blue Ridge. Neill McNeill brought five or six hundred Scotch colonists, landing in Wilmington in 1749, and settling in Bladen, Cumberland and Anson; and again in 1754, and annually thereafter, additions were received to this Colony from Scotland. In 1753 the Moravians, known as the *Unitas Fratrum*, made their settlement between the Dan and Yadkin, and the emigration from the North of Ireland to Pennsylvania, and thence to North Carolina, as well as directly to the latter, was active about the same time.

Although a boundary line had been commenced between North and South Carolina— as had been done in 1727 between Virginia and North Carolina, and had extended to a point on the Pee Dee river, which was extended a few miles further in 1764, the territory west

*Williamson. Vol. II, page 55.

of the Pee Dee was for many years debatable ground so far as jurisdiction was concerned, although it really belonged to the Catawba and Cherokee Indians. These Catawbas and Cherokees were not hostile to the English settlers until tampered with by the French, but were rather friendly disposed to them.

About the beginning of Dobbs's administration in 1754, however, after the French had built Fort Du Quesne, and scattered their emissaries among them, they began to cause apprehension to the settlers on the Western frontiers. In the same year an attempted settlement in that part of the territory beyond the Blue Ridge—which was called in 1776, the District of Washington, in 1784 the State of Franklin, and, finally, in 1796 the State of Tennessee, was defeated and the settlers were driven out. In 1756, Fort Loudon, named for the new British commander-in-chief, the Earl of Loudon, was built about thirty miles from the present city of Knoxville, and a small permanent settlement was made, *which was the first Anglo-American settlement west of the Alleghanies and south of Pennsylvania.*

The Earl of Loudon had not been able, for several reasons, to accomplish much, and he was succeeded in the command of the British forces by General Abercrombie, who began and prosecuted a vigorous campaign against the French. He was repulsed at Ticonderoga but captured Cape Breton and afterwards Fort Frontenac. At the latter place the great loss of ammunition and provisions which the French had accumulated there for use on the Ohio, caused the abandonment of Fort Du Quesne when Forbes's expedition approached that stronghold in 1758, and the communication between their Southern settlements and Canada being thus destroyed, their power on this continent was broken. But, although North Carolina had contributed to the expulsion of the French from Fort Du Quesne, it was only to aggravate her own troubles, for it resulted in transferring French influence and intrigue to the Cherokees on her Western border and kindling anew their animosity, which had been quieted by treaties and acts of conciliation. The result was a series of outbreaks which lasted for more than two years, and which did not leave the settlers in North Carolina in a state of absolute security until the treaty of peace between France and England was made in 1763. Very soon after that event, in 1765, the first rumble of the earthquake which was to rend the British Empire and separate forever the Colonies from the mother country, was heard in the passage of the Stamp Act; and ten years later the great convulsion occurred which established American Independence.

The subject of the following sketch was, from 1755 to 1773, the most conspicuous military figure in the Province of North Carolina, but although mentioned as such in all the histories, no connected account of his life and public services has ever been written.

CHAPTER I.

1754—1757.

GENERAL HUGH WADDELL.

Born in Ireland—His Father's Duel and Flight to America—
Arrival of young Waddell in North Carolina—Enters the
Military Service as Lieutenant in 1754—Makes Treaties
with Indians and Builds Fort Dobbs—Military Services
from 1754 to 1758—A Vindication of Colonel James Innes
and the North Carolina Troops.

HUGH WADDELL was born in Lisburn,
County Down, Ireland. The exact date
of his birth is unknown, but, as it appears from
a memorandum written by his son, and from
a newspaper account of his death, that he was
in his 39th year when he died, April 9th, 1773,
he must have been born in the year 1734 or
early in 1735. He was the son of Hugh Waddell and Isabella Brown, and his ancestors
were among the Scotch emigrants who, in
the previous century, had gone over in large
numbers and settled in the North of Ireland,
and whose descendants in this country were
called Scotch-Irish. The celebrated "blind
preacher" of Virginia, James Waddell, who
was pronounced by Patrick Henry to be the

3

most eloquent man he ever heard, came with
his parents to America from the North of Ireland not long before General Waddell came,
and is believed to have been his near relative.
A highly respected family of the same name
are now residing at Lisburn.

General Waddell's father, who was a choleric
Irish gentleman, about the year 1742 engaged
in a short-sword impromptu duel with another
gentleman of like accommodating spirit and
killed him; and such events having at that
time become so scandalously common in that
country as to have caused the severest enact-
ments against the survivor, the duelist, after
sending for a counsellor and mortgaging (as
he supposed) all his property to him, took his
little boy, then seven or eight years old, and
escaped to America, going to Boston.

Remaining there for several years, and until
the duelling affair was pardoned or forgotten,
and in the meantime providing for the education of his son, he returned with him to Ireland,
only to discover that the counsellor was dead
and that the estate, supposed to have been
mortgaged, had been conveyed absolutely and
had passed into other hands. The authority
for these facts, which is a family tradition,
further says that the counsellor was a relative

of the too confiding duelist, and that the latter was so utterly humiliated and overwhelmed by the double catastrophe that he took to his bed and died. There is an Irish flavor about the tradition which gives it the stamp of truth.

Among the friends of the elder Waddell in Ireland was Arthur Dobbs, a man of considerable culture, who had been a member of the Irish Parliament, and who, in 1741, had suggested the expedition to discover a "northwest passage," which Captain Middleton undertook the next year. Partly because of his supposed enterprising spirit, but chiefly, probably, because of his super-serviceable loyalty to the reigning family and his extravagant notions of the kingly prerogative, Dobbs was, in 1753, appointed Governor of North Carolina, and qualified by taking the oaths of office at Newbern on the first day of November, 1754. Whether he had been in the Province previous to his appointment as Governor, or not, does not appear, but he had, as early as January 14th, 1735, received from Governor Gabriel Johnston a grant for 6,000 acres on the "Largest Branch of Black River," in Dupplin* County (commonly spelled Duplin), and had purchased lands in Anson County from McCulloch.

*So named in honor of Lord Dupplin.

Before Governor Dobbs came over to assume his office, young Waddell had arrived in the Province, having, doubtless, been sent in advance, and arriving in 1753 or early in 1754. He was a Lieutenant in Colonel James Innes' regiment which went to Virginia in the spring of 1754—a full account of which will presently be given—and was made a Captain there.* This was during the administration of Matthew Rowan, President of the Council, who was acting Governor until the arrival of Dobbs, and was the first appearance of Waddell in the history of the Province.†

At the time Dobbs was appointed Governor, the Province was in a condition requiring more than ordinary ability in the Executive, and this ability the aged Governor sadly lacked. When the Legislature assembled, six weeks after his qualification at Newbern, his first recommendation to the body was to fix a permanent and adequate revenue on the Crown to

---

*Governor Dobbs to the Board of Trade. Col. Rec., vol. V, 279; Dinwiddie Papers, vol. I, 367.

†His first civil service was rendered after his return from that expedition, when he was appointed and served for several months as Clerk of the Council, and this writer has two of the original orders of the Council in his handwriting and with his signature attached, dated respectively December 10th, 1754, and January 10th, 1755, which are in a good state of preservation.

meet the expenses of government, and the next was to provide a proper salary for the Governor. The latter suggestion did not seem to excite much enthusiasm among the members of the Legislature, as no notice was taken of it; but they promptly voted eight thousand pounds for the defence of the Province, laid tonnage duties, payable in powder and lead, allowed bounties for facilitating enlistments, and considered and acted upon such other recommendations of the Governor as they deemed important, especially the reorganization of the Court system for the better prevention of crimes, one of which—the counterfeiting of bills of credit—had become an alarming evil. But, although Dobbs was not fully equal to all the requirements of his position, especially in some matters of civil administration, he was prompt and earnest in his efforts to render the Crown all the assistance in his power in the war with the French.

Early in April, 1755, in answer to the request of the ill-fated Braddock, who had, not long before, arrived with his fine English troops at Williamsburg, Va., he met some of the other Governors of the Provinces at Alexandria, where the three celebrated expeditions against Fort Du Quesne, Frontenac and Crown Point

were agreed upon, neither of which was successful, but the last named of which inspired
Dr. Shackburg to compose the tune of Yankee
Doodle.* After his return from the meeting
of the Governors, and during the summer,
Governor Dobbs visited the Western frontier
of North Carolina—as the region around Salisbury was then called—to select sites for the
erection of fortifications, and also made a tour
along the seacoast to ascertain where he could
erect additional forts to those then completed,
or in process of completion, at the mouth of
the Cape Fear River, at Topsail Inlet, at Bear
Inlet and at Ocracoke.† Upon his return, and
at the meeting of the Legislature at Newbern
on the 25th September, he set forth the condition of the Province, the increasing danger of
French supremacy over all the territory west
of the Alleghanies from Canada to Louisiana,
their growing influence over the Indians and

---

*This is the generally accepted origin of Yankee Doodle;
but it is denied, and an interesting history of its origin is given
in "Gleanings for the Curious," page 353.

†The fort at the mouth of the Cape Fear was named Fort
Johnston after Governor Gabriel Johnston, was authorized by
Act of 1745, completed in 1748, made a quarantine station in
1761. Captain John Dalrymple was appointed its commander
by General Braddock in May, 1755. The Fort at Ocracoke was
named Fort Granville.

the necessity for renewed exertions to defeat their schemes. He earnestly appealed to them in the King's name to grant as large a sum as possible, consistent with the resources of the Province, to defend the frontier and to assist in offensive operations against the enemy. He urged, in this connection, the erection of a fort between Third and Fourth Creeks near the South Yadkin River, in Rowan County, which was regarded as nearly a central point on the frontier between the Northern and Southern boundaries of the Province.

In response to this appeal, the Legislature appropriated ten thousand pounds for the erection of the fort at that point, and for raising and equipping and paying three companies of fifty men each, exclusive of commissioned officers.

And now the name of Hugh Waddell began to be conspicuous in North Carolina annals. He had already acquired some reputation, and had been promoted in the expedition of 1754— although not yet of age—as appears, not only from Governor Dobbs' letter already cited, but from the following passage in Williamson's History* in regard to the necessity which arose

*Volume II, page 86.

for treating with the Indians at that time, viz:
"For this purpose, Hugh Waddell, of Rowan
County, an officer of great firmness and integrity, was commissioned to treat with the Catawba and Cherokee Indians." Whether there
is any other reason for giving Rowan County
as his residence at that time than is to be
found in the fact that one of the first grants of
land to him was located there, and that his
military service at that time was rendered there,
is unknown. There is a deed recorded in New
Hanover County for a lot in Wilmington, conveyed by Edward Moseley to his "loving
friend" Hugh Waddell, which is dated "Fort
Dobbs, March 9th, 1761," in which both parties
are described as of Rowan County, but, as
Moseley never lived in Rowan, it is evident
that the place where the deed *was made* is
given as their residence. They were both on
military duty there then, and most of the
grants to Waddell up to that time were for
lands in Anson County.

The treaty referred to by Williamson was
made by Captain Waddell in 1756, about the
time he built the fort authorized by the Assembly in the fall of 1755 above mentioned. It
was a treaty offensive and defensive, and was
executed on behalf of the Catawbas by Ora-

Ioswa, King Higlar and others, and on the part of the Cherokees by the distinguished Chief and Orator, Atta-Kulla-Kulla. This last named Indian Chief was a man of decided ability, and was far in advance of his race in his desire for peace and civilization. He was, according to Hewat, "esteemed to be the wisest man of the nation and the most steady friend of the English." He had visited England as early as 1730,[*] and in 1767 went by sea to New York, where he was treated with marked kindness.[†]

At the instigation of individuals in South Carolina, permitted, if not encouraged, by Governor Lyttleton of that Province, who was constantly doing such things, these Indians demanded, as a part of the treaty, that a fort should be built in the territory of each tribe by the English, as a place of refuge and protection for their women and children in the event that their warriors should have to march against the French.

Virginia and South Carolina built the Chero- kee fort, and North Carolina undertook to build for the Catawbas; but the next year,

*Bancroft, Vol. 348.

†Historical Magazine, Sept., 1857, page 282.

while the workmen were engaged in building
the work, under Captain Waddell's direction,
he was surprised at receiving an order from
Governor Dobbs to discharge them, for the
reason that he, Dobbs, had received a message
from Governor Lyttleton saying that the
Indians desired that no fort should be built
except by South Carolina. Dobbs instructed
Captain Waddell at the same time to inquire
into and ascertain the meaning of such conduct. Where this Catawba Indian fort, intended for their protection, is built is not
known;* but the fort between the Third and
Fourth Creeks, in Rowan, authorized by the
Legislature in 1755, was built by Captain
Waddell previously to his commencing the
work for the Indians and was named Fort
Dobbs. Whether he had any engineering
skill or not does not appear, but very little, if
any, was required in the works erected for
defence against Indian attacks.   In a letter to
the Earl of London, of date July 10th, 1756,
Governor Dobbs, speaking of the necessity for
a fort at Lookout Harbor, says: "As I have
no engineer here, nor know how to get one, I

---

*It is supposed to have been the same as *Old Fort*, in Mc-
Dowell County.

was obliged to act as engineer myself, and rub
up my former knowledge in fortifications when
I was in the army, and have accordingly drawn
up a plan," &c.   A very unique description of
Fort Dobbs was given in the report of the Commissioners, Francis Brown and Richard Caswell, to the Legislature.   They had been sent
out to view the Western settlements, to examine
localities suitable for additional forts, and to
inspect Fort Dobbs, and in regard to the latter
they reported as follows:

"And that they had likewise viewed the
State of Fort Dobbs, and found it to be a good
and Substantial Building of the Dimentions
following (that is to say) The Oblong Square
fifty three feet by forty, the opposite Angles
Twenty four feet and Twenty-Two In height
Twenty four and a half feet as by the Plan
annexed Appears, The Thickness of the Walls
which are made of Oak Logs regularly dimin-
ished from sixteen Inches to Six, it contains
three floors, and there may be discharged from
each floor at one and the same time about one
hundred Musketts the same is beautifully situated in the fork of Fourth Creek a Branch of
the Yadkin River.   And they also found under
Command of Capt Hugh Waddel Forty six
Effective men Officers and Soldiers as by the

List to the said Report Annexed Appears the
same being sworn to by the said Capt in their
Presence the said Officers and Soldiers Appear-
ing well and in good Spirits—Signed the 21st
day of December 1756

Francis Brown
Richard Caswell."

Captain Waddell was twenty-one years old
when this work was erected, and judging by
his rank and the importance of the business
entrusted to him, it is reasonable to suppose
that he had already exhibited the qualities
which afterwards made him the highest military officer in the Province before he had
attained the age of thirty-five.

He remained on frontier duty during the
year 1756, and until the latter part of November, 1757, when he took his seat for the first
time in the General Assembly as a member
from Rowan County, having been elected to
fill a vacancy caused by the expulsion from
that body of a member from that County.
During 1757, in addition to commencing the
fort for the Catawbas which Governor Lyttleton, of South Carolina, interfered with, he was
called upon to make a very long and tedious
march with his command over an exceedingly

rough country to the relief of Fort Loudon,* where Captain Paul Demere† was in great danger. This fort was built by Andrew Lewis under orders from the Earl of Loudon, Commander-in-Chief, and was situated on the Southern bank of the Tennessee River, about thirty miles from the present city of Knoxville, and was the northernmost of a series of forts commencing at Augusta, Georgia, and extending up the Savannah River.

Lewis informed Governor Dobbs that negotiations were going on between the French and the Cherokees, Nantowees and Savannahs, and that after the fort was built, and after Captain Demere, who had been sent there with a garrison of two hundred men, had taken possession, the Cherokees expressed great dissatisfaction at the presence of so many armed men among them and desired that they should be sent back. Lewis said their intention was to take the fort and surrender it to the French. Upon this information Captain Waddell was sent out with reinforcements.‡

*There was also a Fort Loudon at Winchester, Virginia.

†Mis-spelled Dennie in all N. C. histories. He was Captain of the South Carolina Independent Company after Captain MacKaye. Commanded at Fort Prince George in 1760, and was killed by the Cherokees.

‡Martin, vol. II, page 90.

An examination of a map of the country over which this march had to be made, will give some idea of the kind of service required of Provincial troops at that time. The distance by the route taken was more than two hundred miles, the whole territory was covered by an unbroken forest, and nearly half of it was a wilderness of mountain ranges higher than any on the continent east of the Rocky Mountains. There were no roads except Indian trails, and no inhabitants save the savage and treacherous red man.

Again, during the year 1757, Governor Dobbs was asked to render aid to South Carolina where, as Governor Lyttleton informed him, the Indians, continually instigated by the French, were becoming very troublesome and would soon, unless aid was extended, be beyond his power to control. The Legislature granted the aid asked, and it is probable that Captain Waddell was again ordered to march his command to the relief of the sister Colony, but there is no record of the expedition.

He remained on frontier duty, as already stated, until elected to the Assembly, in which body he took his seat on the 28th November, 1757, and on the adjournment of the Assembly he returned to his command, and soon after, in May, 1758, was promoted to the rank of Major, and assigned to the command of the three companies raised for the final expedition against Fort Du Quesne under General Forbes, an account of which will be given in the next chapter.

Before proceeding to an account of that expedition, however, it will be alike pertinent to the subject, and eminently due to the memory of another brave and faithful North Carolina Colonial officer, to recite the facts in regard to the campaign of 1754, with which he, and the soldiers under him, were connected, and concerning which there has been some mystification and much misrepresentation. The publication, in 1884, of the "Dinwiddie Papers" by the Historical Society of Virginia, has thrown much light on the subject, although if both sides of the correspondence between Governor Dinwiddie and that officer could have been preserved and published, the facts would be much clearer than they are.

At the beginning of the year 1754, while Matthew Rowan, President of the Council, was acting Governor of North Carolina, and before the arrival of Governor Dobbs, the Assembly

had voted—as they always did, though other
Colonies failed*—a liberal sum of money
(£12,000) in aid of Virginia to repel French
invasion and maintain the right of Great Britain
to the territory along the Ohio and its tributa-
ries. This was the *first time* in our Colonial
history that troops were raised by a Colony
*to serve outside of its borders in the common
defence of all*, and the spirit thereby manifested
exhibited itself afterwards in the *first armed*
resistance to the Stamp Act in America, and
in the *first Declaration* of Independence.

On the 23d of March Governor Dinwiddie
acknowledged the receipt of a letter from President Rowan, by the hands of Mr. Ashe, in
regard to the action of North Carolina, and
expressed his pleasure thereat. He said his
own Assembly were much divided, that a spirit
of contention existed among them, and that
they had voted only £10,000 for the immediate raising of 300 men to join and escort a
company of 100 men, then on the Ohio, for
the purpose of building a fort; but he did not
doubt that they would raise a much larger
sum for the general defence. He said that as

---

* "Except North Carolina, not one of the other Colonies has
granted any supplies." Governor Dinwiddie to C. Hanbury,
May 10th, 1754.

the campaign was to be for the common safety
of all, each Colony should pay and provision
its own forces. He expressed surprise at the
liberal pay allowed by North Carolina to her
soldiers, viz.: three shillings a day, and begged
President Rowan to use his influence with the
officers and soldiers to induce them to accept
the same pay as the Virginians, which was
eight pence a day, but said he feared, if the
North Carolinians knew that, they would not
come. Then, after some inquiry about provisions, Governor Dinwiddie says:

"I am glad your regiment comes under the
command of Colonel Innes, whose capacity,
judgment and cool conduct I have a great
regard for. And when he comes here I will
do all I can to help him. The march of your
people by land will be long and very fatiguing.
I advise their coming by sea to Hampton," &c.

On the same day he wrote to Colonel Innes,
in answer to a letter from him by Mr. Ashe,
addressing him as "Dear James," expressing
his pleasure at the prospect of seeing him "at
the head of a regiment of 750 men," telling
him that he intended him for the chief command, but that the few troops already raised
had to march immediately to the Ohio, and,
therefore, he had to commission the officers.

4

It would seem that Colonel Innes had alluded
to his own age as a possible difficulty in his
way, and also to the expectations of the Virginians in regard to the command of the troops,
for Governor Dinwiddie says : "Your age is
nothing when you reflect on your regular
method of living." And again: "As for the
expectations of the people here, I always have
regard to merit, and I know yours, and you
need not mind or fear any reflections."

Colonel Innes reported in person to Governor Dinwiddie promptly, and on the 15th
April, took a letter from him to President
Rowan, from which it appears that there had
been a full conference between them in regard
to the North Carolina forces.

Colonel Joshua Fry, "an English gentleman, bred at Oxford,"* was made Commander-
in-Chief of the expedition. Lieutenant Colonel
George Washington started from Alexandria
on the 10th May with the first detachment of
150 men, and had arrived within seventy-five
miles of the place selected for the erection of
the fort at the Forks of the Monongahela, when
he learned that a French force had come down
on the company building it and had captured it.

---

*Montcalm and Wolfe, by Francis Parkman, Vol. I, 142.

Washington then went into camp and awaited reinforcements. Colonel Fry was taken ill, and there was great delay in moving his command to Washington's assistance. About the first of June Colonel Fry died, and on the 4th Governor Dinwiddie, writing to Washington, whom he had promoted to the Colonelcy of the Virginia regiment in Fry's stead, informed him that " Colonel James Innes, an old experienced officer, is daily expected, who is appointed Commander-in-Chief of all the forces, which I am very sensible will be very agreeable to you and the other officers." On the same day he made out Colonel Innes' commission as Commander-in-Chief, and his instructions. On the 10th, Washington, acknowledging the receipt of the letter to him, says: "I rejoice that I am likely to be happy under the command of an experienced officer and man of sense. It is what I have ardently wished for." On the 20th, Governor Dinwiddie, writing to the Governor of New York, announced the arrival of the two companies from that Province, but complained bitterly that they were not only not " Compleat in Numbers," as promised, but that many were too old to stand a march of two hundred miles; that they had no blankets, tents or provisions, and were " burthened with thirty women and children"—a decidedly Falstaffian combination.

About the last of June, the North Carolina troops, which, upon the discovery that each of the Colonies would have to support its own forces, had been reduced in number from 750, the force originally determined upon, to 450, began to arrive at Winchester, having marched through the country instead of taking ship to Hampton, as suggested by Governor Dinwiddie, and about the same time Colonel Washington was complaining to the Governor that his command had had no flour for six days, and could not hear of any on the way to them; that they did not have provisions of any sort for two days ahead, and that they were in want of ammunition.

Colonel Innes was also writing to Governor Dinwiddie about the wretched mismanagement of the expedition and the want of supplies of all sorts; and, finally, on the 11th of July, he informed him that unless something was done he should disband the North Carolina regiment and let them go home. They were not only without supplies, but their pay was in arrears and they could not buy what they needed. Governor Dinwiddie declined to advance any money to them, saying, "Our own regiment

has got all the money I can spare," and repeat-
ing that each Colony must subsist its own
forces. He said he and the Quartermaster and
Commissary were in advance to the North
Carolina regiment, *and expected payment from
the produce of the pork brought from North
Carolina*, or purchased by Innes, and he advised
the latter to consult Governor Dobbs as to
what he should do for the future, "and it is
probable he will find some method of keeping
your regiment together for eight months
longer." After telling him to call a council
of officers to consult about building a log fort
and magazine, and saying that he did not wish
him to proceed towards the Ohio, &c., &c., he
again informs him as follows: "I can give no
orders for entertaining your regiment, as this
Dominion will maintain none but their own
forces." At the same time, as appears by
Governor Dinwiddie's letter to Abercrombie, he
was supplying the two independent companies
from New York, and the independent company
from South Carolina, with everything they
needed, except their pay, which came out of
the royal revenue, viz.: "tents, blankets, ket-
tles, knapsacks, spatterdashes, wagons and
provisions," and the South Carolina company
had gone to the front and joined Washington,

and on the 3d of July had surrendered, with the force under him, at the Great Meadows, after a gallant engagement with much superior numbers.

Colonel Innes, who was at Winchester, where the forces were to assemble, soon discovered a strong feeling among the Virginians against his appointment to the chief command, and a mutinous disposition soon developed itself among them, which he reported to the Governor, who said he was sorry for it, and added that they had been greatly fatigued and not properly paid, "but as money is ordered for them I hope they will proceed with spirit."

The North Carolina troops were not recruited rapidly, and, from various causes, were slow in getting to Virginia. They were, doubtless, apprehensive of the very result which happened. Knowing that their number had been reduced from that originally intended, because of the difficulty of supporting such a force beyond the limits of the Province, where the only money they had would not pass current, they doubtless began the service with misgivings. Finding after they got to Virginia that they were in danger of starvation, and that the Virginians were mutinous about Colonel Innes' appointment, and that Governor Dinwiddie demanded that they should not receive more than eight pence a day, and that he had written to Colonel Innes " they cannot have the impudence to expect more than eight pence a day, as the other forces have, and if you cannot compel them to serve for it I think they had better be disbanded," and Governor Dinwiddie having expressed the opinion, *in advance* of any knowledge on the subject, that their company officers were incompetent, and the situation having become well-nigh desperate under the pressure of such circumstances, Colonel Innes disbanded them.

These are the facts in regard to this matter, as gathered from the correspondence of Governor Dinwiddie himself, recently published, but they do not so appear upon the page of history. There the North Carolina troops are represented (as one writer puts it) as having "disbanded themselves in a very disorderly manner," and "to this unmilitary conduct and lack of patriotism " is attributed the failure of the projected expedition against the French.* None of the reasons for their conduct are given, except such as make them appear in an unfavorable light.

---

*Sparks's " Washington's Writings," Vol. II, page 63, note.

Colonel Innes was ordered to build a fort on
Wills's Creek, afterwards called Fort Cumberland, as a rallying point, and did so. He
remained there in command with about 400
men, only forty of whom were North Carolinians.

The Virginia Assembly met on the 22d day
of August, and on the 27th passed a supply
bill for £20,000, but the next day put a "rider"
on it, to pay a private account, greatly to the
disgust of Governor Dinwiddie, who called it
"a rider" in a letter to Governor Hamilton,
and said in a letter to Lord Fairfax, "I imagine
your Lordship, in your observation of the Parliament's proceedings, does not remember any
tack to a money bill since King William's
reign."

The Council rejected the bill thus clogged,
and as the House stuck to their "rider" the
Governor prorogued them until the 17th October. This refusal to vote money to support
the troops, although ostensibly because of the
failure of the "rider," was really because
Colonel Innes was occupying the position
which the Assembly thought Washington
ought to have, and, consequently, there was no
attempt at a movement against the French.

Colonel Innes became very restive under his

enforced inaction and the many annoyances to
which he was subjected, and so informed the
Governor, who begged him to be patient a little
while longer. This was on the 5th of October.

Between that date and the 20th, Governor
Dinwiddie, Governor Dobbs, the newly appointed Governor of North Carolina, and Governor Sharpe of Maryland met for consultation
and agreed upon a plan of operations ; and at
this meeting Governor Sharpe produced a commission from the King appointing him Commander-in-Chief of the proposed expedition,
whereupon the Governors agreed to appoint
Colonel Innes "Camp Master General" with
the rank then held by him, and he was so
notified on the 24th. On the 25th, Governor
Dinwiddie, writing to Sir Thomas Robinson,
said he was glad Governor Sharpe was appointed
Commander-in-Chief, as it would put an end
to some disputes between the independent
companies and the officer in command.

"This person, Colonel J. Innes," he said,
"has been in His Majesty's army and is of
an unblemished character, of great reputation
for his bravery and conduct, and I shall still
endeavor to keep him in the service."

Innes wanted to resign, and Washington
did resign, on account of the impudent claims

of the Captains of the independent companies, who refused to recognize their superior rank.

Governor Sharpe never had an opportunity to display his military skill that year, and the next year Braddock was sent out from England as commander of the forces.

Colonel Innes remained at Fort Cumberland making treaties with the Indians and organizing the forces while completing the fort; and on the 24th June, 1755, was appointed "Governor of Fort Cumberland" by General Braddock, and left in command there when Braddock advanced on his hapless march. And there he received the broken fugitives from the fatal field, and there he was abandoned by Colonel Dunbar, who succeeded Braddock in the command, and who precipitately "went into winter-quarters" (in August) in Philadelphia, leaving Innes with 400 sick and wounded, and a handful of Provincials to defend the frontier. And there this ill-used but true and loyal soldier continued to do his duty to his King and country faithfully and in the face of all sorts of difficulties until the spring of 1756, when he returned to North Carolina on leave of absence.

Sparks, in a note to his edition of Washington's Writings (Vol. II, page 262), says that Colonel Innes was incompetent, and that, aside from his incompetency, he was an inhabitant of North Carolina, and, as such, was unacceptable to the Virginia troops, and that Governor Dinwiddie was censured on the ground that he was partial to Innes because he and Innes were both natives of Scotland. The charge of incompetency was not supported by any evidence whatever, unless Colonel Innes' patient endurance of ungenerous treatment, his urgent requests to be sent to the front, and the commendation of Governor Dinwiddie, and Lord Loudon, the Commander-in-Chief, can be twisted into such evidence. He had served as a Captain in the expedition against Carthagena in 1740, and was an intimate friend of Washington's elder brother, Major Lawrence Washington, who was also a Captain in Colonel Wm. Gooch's Virginia regiment in that affair.

That he was not the equal of Washington may be cordially admitted, but it is to be remembered that, at that time, Washington himself had been the victim of two disasters— the surrender at the Great Meadows and Braddock's defeat—and that no opportunity had been presented for the exhibition of his great capacity; and further, that, however absurd a

comparison between him and Washington may
now appear, the situation then did not justify
Mr. Sparks' criticism, which is thus com-
mented upon because it was the basis upon
which many, if not all, subsequent writers have
rested their discussion of the campaigns of
1754–'55. Mr. Sparks was entirely justified,
however, in characterizing as natural* the assertion of their "rights" in the affair by the
Virginians, for three years afterwards the
Virginia Assembly, being dissatisfied with the
manner in which Forbes' expedition was managed, "and with the partiality which they
imagined was shown to Pennsylvania," passed
an act on the 14th of September, 1758, to withdraw the first regiment (Washington's) from
the Regulars on the 1st December and station
it on the frontiers of their own Colony—which
would have amounted to a withdrawal of all
the Virginia troops, as the time of enlistment
of the *second* regiment expired on the 1st of
December, while the first regiment was enlisted
for the war.

The foregoing narrative of facts, which is
now for the first time compiled, is given in
justice to the memory of a good and true man,

---

*Sparks, Vol. II, page 308, note.

who died a childless benefactor of the children
of his poorer fellow-citizens. And as a proper
conclusion to it, the following biographical
data are added:

James Innes was born, as is inferred from a
clause in his will, at Cannisbay, in Caithness,
which is in the extreme Northern part of Scotland, near "John O'Groat's house." He probably came to the Province of North Carolina
with Governor Gabriel Johnston, as he was
recommended for appointment to the Council
in 1734, and was living in the Province in 1735.
He was a member of the Council from July,
1750, to May, 1759, having previously served
as Captain in the expedition to Carthagena,
and having been one of Lord Granville's agents,
and Colonel of the New Hanover militia. He
died on the 5th of September, 1759, at Wilmington. By his will, which was made July
5th, 1754, at Winchester, Va., which was proved
before Governor Dobbs at Newbern, October
9th, 1759, and is registered in New Hanover
County, Colonel Innes, after directing that a
remittance may be made "to Edinburg sufficient
to pay for a church bell for the Parish Church at
Cannisbay, in Caithness," and a further remittance of one hundred pounds sterling, to be
put at interest for the poor of said Parish, gave

his plantation, "Point Pleasant," near Wilmington, a considerable personal estate, his library and one hundred pounds sterling " for the use of a free school for the benefit of the youth of North Carolina," and appointed as trustees of the fund "the Coll: (Colonel) of New Hanover regiment, the Parson of Wilmington Church, and the Vestry for the time being, or the majority of them." *This was the first private bequest for educational purposes in the history of North Carolina*, and in the same year (1754) the first appropriation by the Legislature for a public seminary was made. The Trustees, under his will, recovered very little of his property, the houses having been burned, but the " Innes Academy " was started under an act of the Legislature of 1783, and was kept up for some time by private subscription.

Colonel Innes' widow Jean, in 1761, married Francis Corbin, Lord Granville's agent, a member of the Council, who was removed therefrom in 1760.

CHAPTER II.

1758–1764.

Forbes' Expedition to Fort Du Quesne—Major Waddell Commands the North Carolina Troops—Sergeant John Rogers—Return of the North Carolina Troops and Expedition Against the Cherokees—Waddell promoted to a Colonelcy—Peace Declared—End of Dobbs' Administration—Notice of Dobbs' Family.

THE forces on Braddock's expedition in 1755, numbered about two thousand, one-half of whom were Provincial troops, and of these North Carolina furnished less than one hundred, under Dobbs' son, Edward Brice Dobbs, as Major. These North Carolinians were not engaged in Braddock's fight, but were with the reserve corps under Dunbar. The other half of Braddock's army was composed of two regiments of British Regulars from Ireland, the 44th and 48th, numbering five hundred men each, and commanded respectively by Sir Peter Halket and Colonel Dunbar. These regiments, which were said to be equal to any in the British army, were accompanied by an artillery train and military supplies.

The terrible disaster which befell the expedition is familiar to every reader of American history, and a touching account of the discovery of the remains of Sir Peter Halket and his young son who fought by his side, when Forbes' expedition reached the battlefield three years afterwards, is given by Bancroft.

The expedition of 1758, under General Forbes, was more than three times as large as Braddock's, and consisted of 1,200 Highlanders, 350 Royal Americans—a specially organized corps—about 2,700 Pennsylvanians, 1,600 Virginians, 250 Marylanders, and three companies of North Carolinians, with whom were some Indians.

Braddock's expedition ended in an awful butchery and a disgraceful panic and flight of the British Regulars, which the heroic conduct of Washington and his Provincials could not avail to arrest.

Forbes' expedition terminated, after six months of terrible hardships, in the occupation of the smoking ruins of a fort from which the enemy had fled.

There is, to the reader of the present day, a profound pathos in the letters of Washington, written during the period covered by these two expeditions.

The constant and numerous difficulties and

annoyances to which he was subjected on the
last one, and which ranged from building camp
chimneys for the General, or regulating the
steelyards of a contractor, all the way through
the category of defending himself from slander,
resisting impudent attempts to degrade him in
rank, or passing sleepless nights of anxiety
over the condition of his troops and the fate of
the expedition, up to the time when, writing
from Loyal Hanna to Governor Fauquier, he
says: "The General and great part of his
troops being yet behind, and the weather growing very inclement, I apprehend our expedition
must terminate for this year at this place."
These trials and the emotions they excited in
him are all faithfully reflected in his correspondence during that period, which was carefully preserved and published, with his other
writings, nearly a half century after his death.
These letters discover the same calm and lofty
spirit, the same sturdy sense of duty, the same
self-poise, the same courage and sagacity, and
the same inflexible integrity which marked his
whole career and made his name immortal.

In the spring of 1758, when the preliminary
arrangements for Forbes' expedition were in
progress, Major Waddell was assigned to the
command of the three North Carolina compa-

5

nies authorized to be recruited by the act of Assembly granting aid to the expedition, in answer to Mr. Pitt's appeal to the Colonies. He at once proceeded to organize, equip and prepare the troops for their long march, and as soon as they were ready he set out with them for Virginia.

There was no complaint of delay in his getting to the front, as there had been frequently by Governor Dinwiddie in regard to the North Carolina forces in the two previous expeditions of 1754 and 1755. He marched promptly to Virginia and went thence to the front immediately. The writer of these pages now has a field return made by Major Wad-·dell on that expedition. It is written on a sheet about eight inches in length by five inches in breadth, in a very clear, legible hand, and although the paper is somewhat worn and discolored, the ink is comparatively fresh-looking. It is headed: "A Field Return of the North Carolina Detachment under the command of Major Waddell, Loyal Hannon,* 25th October 1758." Besides the officers, there are but twenty-six men on the return, but imme-

---

*Governor Dinwiddie spelled this name "Loyal henning." It is Loyal Hanna.

diately under it, and before his signature, "Hu Waddell Maj: N. C. Troops," there is an addition of the figures 26 and 96, and a footing of 122, which was, doubtless, his effective force. The date and place of this field return fully corroborate the statement afterwards made by Governor Dobbs, that Major Waddell "had great honor done him, being employed on all reconnoitering parties" on this expedition.

One of those minor events which so often shape history, but are lost sight of in general results, occurred to Major Waddell's command on this expedition; but, although—as has been the case with so many more important facts in the history of North Carolina—no credit has ever been given for it, it is nevertheless true that the North Carolina companies were in the advance corps of Forbes's army, scouting, reconnoitering, clearing roads, building bridges and boats, and rendering the most valuable service; and that to a Sergeant of Major Waddell's command, named John Rogers,* General Forbes was indebted for the information which caused the immediate advance and occupation

---

*At August Term, 1765, the Inferior Court of New Hanover County, of which General Waddell was a Magistrate, appointed John Rogers a Constable.

of the fort. They had been in the advance corps from the beginning, and before Washington had, upon his own earnest application,* been assigned to that command. This is evident, from the fact that Major Waddell's field return, already mentioned, is dated at Loyal Hanna on the 25th October, while Colonel Washington did not reach that point in the advance until the 30th.

Washington, who had saved the remnant of Braddock's expedition three years before, although treated with great consideration and freely consulted by General Forbes, was greatly apprehensive that the persistent refusal to act upon his advice would defeat the purpose of the expedition, as appears by his letter of September 1st to Speaker Robinson, in which he said: "Nothing now but a miracle can bring this campaign to a happy issue." When, finally, the accumulating obstacles, delays and

---

*"Colonel Stephen gives me some room to apprehend that a body of light troops may soon move on. I pray your interest most sincerely with the General to get my regiment and myself included in the number. If any argument is needed to obtain this favor, I hope, without vanity, I may be allowed to say, that from long intimacy with these woods, and frequent scouting in them, my men are at least as well acquainted with all the passes and difficulties as any troops that will be employed." Washington to Colonel Bouquet, 21 July.

embarrassments culminated in a council of war, at which the alternative was presented of going into winter quarters or abandoning the expedition, "a mere accident," as Sparks says, occurred, which "brought hope out of despair." This mere accident, which all the historians mention, and to which Washington himself alludes as a Providential occurrence, but without mentioning any names, was the capture of an Indian from whom the true situation of affairs at Fort Du Quesne was learned. But although this mere accident, or, in other words, this event of absolutely vital importance to the success of this formidable expedition, which established English supremacy in the South, is carefully recorded, the person who was so fortunate as to accomplish this mere accident is as carefully ignored, to-wit, Sergeant John Rogers of the North Carolina forces. It was a little thing to do, perhaps, but Forbes considered the importance of doing it so great that he offered a reward of fifty guineas, and another officer offered a reward of four hundred guineas[*] to any one who would take an Indian prisoner, so that they might get infor-

---

[*] Petition of John Rogers to the Assembly. Colonial Records of N. C., Vol. VI, 384.

mation of the enemy's movements. Rogers accomplished it at the hazard of his life, and from the prisoner captured by him it was ascertained that the garrison at Fort Du Quesne were only waiting the appearance of the British when they would withdraw, and thereupon the light troops made a forced march and the enemy burned and abandoned the fort.

General Forbes died without paying or providing for the payment of the reward to Rogers, but the Assembly of North Carolina allowed him twenty pounds for his gallantry.

Major Waddell himself "dressed and acted as an Indian" on this expedition, according to Governor Dobbs's statement, and a tradition in his family says that a large dog belonging to him was the first living creature that entered Fort Du Quesne after the French evacuated it.

After the fall of the fort all the troops, except enough to garrison it, returned to their homes, including the North Carolinians.

But the French, who retired from Fort Du Quesne and moved farther southward, very soon had an opportunity to retaliate, and form an alliance with the very same Cherokees who had been co-operating with the English. This was the result of an unfortunate, and, as it

turned out, a cruel act on the part of some
Virginians.

The Cherokees had aided the British on
every expedition against Fort Du Quesne,
strictly adhering in this respect to their treaty
obligations; and it was on the return of the
warriors from this final expedition that the
unfortunate occurrence referred to took place.
They were passing through the extreme frontier settlements of Virginia, and finding some
horses running wild in the woods—as was the
case everywhere on the frontiers—they took
some of them to supply the places of those
they had lost on the expedition, "never im-
agining," as is said by Hewat, "that they
belonged to any individual in the Province."
Thereupon some Virginians, without attempting any other process of redress, attacked them
with arms and killed twelve or fourteen of
the unsuspecting warriors and took others
prisoners. The Cherokees were naturally
incensed at such an ungrateful and cruel
return from the people whose soil they had
marched several hundred miles to defend, and
when they reached their homes at once told
what had happened. The result was an out-

burst of fury, especially among the young warriors who were kinsmen of the victims; and the emissaries of the French, who were among them, added fuel to the flame of their resentment by telling them that the British intended to kill all their warriors and to reduce all their women and children to slavery. These emissaries roused their vengeance in every way and supplied them with arms and ammunition. Fort Loudon, on the Tennessee, where there was a garrison of 200 men under Captains Demere and Stuart, was one of the first objects of their vengeance, and hunting parties and stragglers from that post were attacked and killed. Descents were made upon the settlements and the inhabitants were murdered and scalped. Fort Loudon was cut off from supplies and the garrison was in danger of starvation.[*]

The news of the Cherokee outbreak soon spread and reached Fort Prince George, near the upper Savannah river, whose commanding officer notified the Governor of South Carolina. Governor Dobbs was also notified, and at once ordered Waddell, who had been promoted to the rank of Colonel, to take all the Provincial

---

[*]Carr, Coll. I, 444.

troops, and all the militia of Orange, Anson and Rowan Counties, who could be properly armed, and rendezvous at Fort Prince George in conjunction with an expedition fitted out by Governor Lyttleton, of South Carolina and numbering about 1,400 men. The militia refused to march against the Cherokees, upon the ground that they were not bound to serve out of the limits of the Province. Colonel Waddell notified Governor Dobbs of this, and sent him, by the same express, a letter he had received from Governor Lyttleton. Dobbs appealed to the Assembly, then in session (Nov. 26th, 1759), and asked them to "pass a short bill to explain and enforce the militia law, and oblige the militia to act where ordered for the public good and the defence of the Province." On the 29th November the Assembly ordered about a thousand pounds to be given to Colonel Waddell to buy wagons, &c., and a resolution was passed "that the forces now in the pay of this Province, and the militia thereof, not to exceed 500 men," be kept in pay until the 10th February, if necessary, and appropriated five thousand pounds therefor.

The Cherokees were overawed by this display of force and begged for peace. Another treaty was made with them, one of the provisions of which required them to leave twenty-four hostages, to secure the delivery of twenty-four Indians who had murdered the same number of whites since the former treaty.

Governor Lyttleton very unwisely withdrew his forces, leaving only a small guard over the hostages, and the result was an attempt by the Indians to surprise the garrison and rescue the hostages on the 27th January, 1760.[*] They failed, but they murdered some traders and held the fort under a close blockade for some time.

Colonel Waddell's force had been reduced after the treaty, but, upon a new outbreak of the Indians, he re-garrisoned Fort Dobbs and, under instructions, put five hundred militia on duty to protect the frontiers. He was attacked by the Indians at Fort Dobbs on the evening of the 27th February, the assault being made by two parties, but he repulsed them, killing ten or twelve, and lost only one boy killed and two men wounded, one of whom was scalped.[†]   He expected an attack the next

*Williamson, Vol. II, 93.   Carr, Col. I, 451.

†His name was Robert Campbell, and he was allowed by the Assembly twenty pounds for "present subsistence." Col. Rec., Vol. VI, 422.

night, but the Indians had enough of it and did not make another attempt.

Whether Colonel Waddell was with the expedition of Colonel Montgomery and Major Grant which invaded the Cherokee country and fought an indecisive battle in the Etchoe settlement, near the present town of Franklin, on the 27th June, is uncertain. The retreat of Montgomery to Fort Prince George caused the surrender of Fort Loudon, which was followed by treachery and murder by the Indians.

In the fall, however, Colonel Waddell was ordered to join Colonel Byrd, of Virginia, in striking the upper Cherokees, but the latter made peace and he discharged his troops.

Thus the first five years after his arrival in the Province were passed by Colonel Waddell chiefly in the field in active service against the French and Indians.

There is no record of any special service rendered by him between the years 1760 and 1765, except that which he performed during the sessions of the Assembly, of which body he was a prominent and useful member. As the population of the Province was steadily increasing, especially in the Western portion, and the Indian depredations were gradually ceasing, until the peace between Great Britain

and France in 1763 put a stop to them entirely,
it is most probable that he was relieved from
active duty, and began to utilize the advan-
tages, which his experience and knowledge of
the country gave him, by judicious investments
in lands, and the establishment of "stores"
in various places in the back country, where
the certainty of large profits awaited such
ventures. That he did this about that time,
and that he was largely interested in the mercantile firm of John Burgwin & Co., and
realized handsome profits from the business, is
known. He married in 1762, and Mr. Burgwin's association with him in business was
attributable to the fact that their wives were
sisters and co-heiresses.

Governor Dobbs, who was about seventy
years old when he was appointed Governor,
because of his age, his infirmities of tempera-
ment, and his ultra loyalty and unreasonable
ideas in regard to prerogative, had not only
irritated and disgusted the people, but had
worn out the patience of his best friends; and,
in October, 1764, Lieutenant Colonel William
Tryon, of the Queen's Guards, was sent over
and qualified as Lieutenant Governor of the
Province at Wilmington.

In the following March, Governor Dobbs

died, in his 82d year, and was buried on his plantation on Town Creek, below Wilmington. He had obtained a leave of absence, and intended going to England when death overtook him.

In a letter to the Earl of Halifax, dated April 2d, 1765, at Wilmington, Tryon writes as follows:

"Last Thursday Governor Dobbs retired from the strife and cares of this world. Two days before his death he was busily employed in packing up his books for his passage to England. His physician had no other means to prevent his fatiguing himself than by telling him he had better prepare himself for a much longer voyage."

The poor old man departed at a good time for himself, and, doubtless, at a convenient season for his lively and handsome young widow, who, not long afterwards, consoled herself with a new and younger husband, who was also destined, but under very different auspices, to be Governor of North Carolina, namely, Abner Nash.

Governor Dobbs was a widower when he came to North Carolina, and he came solely for the purpose of improving his fortunes and providing for his near relatives—objects in the

pursuit of which he cannot be accused of a
want of diligence.

By his first marriage he had two sons and
two daughters, none of whom, except his
younger son, accompanied him to this country.
His oldest son, Conway Richard Dobbs, became
High Sheriff of County Antrim, and the family
seat, called Castle Dobbs, is still in the possession of his descendants.* His second son,
Edward Brice Dobbs, was appointed Captain
of the North Carolina company sent on Braddock's expedition ; was afterwards, in the New
York expedition, made a Major; was a member
of the Council of North Carolina in 1757, and
in 1767 signed himself " Captain in H. M.'s
7th Regt of Foot or Royal Fusiliers."

Governor Dobbs's second wife was Justina
Davis, a daughter of John Davis, Esq., a
planter living near Brunswick, on Cape Fear
River. They had no child, and after Dobbs's
death she married Abner Nash, who was a
Major in the Revolution—a brother of General
Francis Nash, who was killed at Germantown—
was afterwards Governor of North Carolina,
and was the father of the late Chief Justice
Nash.

*Dinwiddie Papers.

When the trouble arose about the attachment law of the Province, which, like the
attachment laws of several other Provinces,
gave a resident creditor advantage over all
others by subjecting the property of non-resi-
dent debtors to seizure for the satisfaction of
such resident creditor's claim, one of the leading cases arising under the act was that of
Abner Nash against the Dobbs estate, in 1773,
in which an attachment had been levied on
the interest of Dobbs's son, who lived in Ireland, to satisfy a legacy of £2,000 left by
Dobbs's will to his widow. The case went
before the Privy Council and the plaintiff
gained it.

Governor Dobbs also brought over with him
his nephew, Richard Spaight, who was made
paymaster to the North Carolina forces in
Braddock's expedition, was Secretary of the
Province in 1756, and a member of the Council.
He was the father of Richard Dobbs Spaight,
who was Governor of North Carolina in 1792,
and who was killed in a duel by John Stanly
in 1802, and was the grandfather of the second
Richard Dobbs Spaight, who was also Governor in 1834.

Throughout the whole of Dobbs's adminisistration, Colonel Waddell appears to have been the most prominent military figure in the Province, and to have enjoyed the respect and confidence of both authorities and people in a high degree.

CHAPTER III.

1765.

Tryon Becomes Governor—His Character and Conduct—The Stamp Act—Arrival of the Sloop of War Diligence at Brunswick—Colonel Waddell, with Colonel Ashe and others, Resists the Landing of the Stamps.

UPON the death of Governor Dobbs, Tryon succeeded to the Governorship and qualified on the 3d April, 1765.

He was an accomplished man of the world and a gallant soldier, but he was also vain and imperious. He still retained his rank in the British army and his place in the regular line of promotion, and he was ambitious of distinction in the administration of a Colonial government in which there had been, for many years, continual disagreement between the Assembly and his predecessors, and growing dissatisfaction among the people with their local civil officers.

So far as their relations with the Crown were concerned, the inhabitants of the Province of North Carolina were as loyal as its most loyal subjects anywhere, but they had, particularly

6

in the Western part of the Province, been annoyed, irritated and oppressed by the petty frauds and extortions practiced upon them by entry-takers, deputy surveyors, land agents and court officers, and by the failure, in many cases, of their own Assembly to provide adequate remedies for these evils.

The character of Governor Tryon was totally different from that of Governor Dobbs. He was more adroit and conciliatory, and while cherishing high ideas of prerogative, was free from the little infirmities which age had only emphasized in Dobbs. He was passionate, but his passion was under control; he was young and vigorous, but—beyond a desire to display some "pomp and circumstance," and to live luxuriously—was not disposed to harry or oppress the people. His appointment to the office of Governor was, however, made at an unfortunate time for himself. The Stamp Act, a veritable Pandora's box, and the most far-reaching legislative blunder in the history of England, was passed by Parliament and received the Royal sanction about a fortnight before he qualified as Dobbs's successor,*

---

*The Stamp Act was approved March 22d, and he qualified April 3d.

and the news of its passage, which had been anticipated, was not long in getting to America.

Before the passage of the Stamp Act, the Parliament of Great Britain had, in 1764, for the first time,* undertaken to appropriate the property of American subjects to the purpose of increasing the revenues of the Crown by imposing a duty on sugar, coffee, wine and other articles of foreign growth imported into the Colonies. Finding that there was still a deficit in the revenues, after the imposition of these duties on foreign imports, and in pursuance of a previously declared purpose, they passed the Stamp Act in 1765.

This act, which has already been characterized as the most far-reaching legislative blunder in the history of England, was the pet project of George Grenville, Chancellor of the Exchequer, who had adopted the plan of taxation from Lord Bute, to whom it had been suggested by Jenkinson.

The act, which contained fifty-five sections, provided an elaborate system of stamp duties for the Colonies, and all offences against its provisions were made cognizable in the Courts of Admiralty, in which there were no juries, "so that the Americans were not only to be

*Bancroft, Vol. V, 188.

taxed by the British Parliament, but to have
the taxes collected arbitrarily, under the decree
of British Judges, without any trial by jury."*

In introducing the measure, Grenville made
an adroit and plausible speech, as he had done
when, unfolding the budget of the previous
year, he gave notice of his intention to bring
in the present bill; but he did not find the
same unanimity in favor of the latter, for
while there was no debate and not one negative
on the passage of the bill of 1764, the Stamp
Act was debated for some time with much
animation, and, on its final passage, forty-two
votes were recorded against it, to two hundred
and ninety-four in its favor.

The opponents of the bill, however, almost
without exception, admitted the power of Parliament to pass the measure, although its con-
stitutionality was as bitterly denied in the
Colonies as the injustice of its provisions, and
the utter inability of the people to comply with
them was earnestly asserted. The measure
was not only a new one, but threatened ruin
to the Colonies. It was an internal revenue
bill, exclusively applicable to the Colonies,
which were without representation in the body

*Bancroft (quoting Walpole), Vol. V, 156.

that enacted it, and it clogged every transaction of a business nature requiring the use
of paper, and taxed the privilege of publishing,
advertising in, or reading newspapers, pamphlets and other publications. The tax, too,
was not only imposed upon a multiplicity of
objects, but was very heavy on each. The
cheapest stamp was one shilling. It taxed
knowledge as well as business. The tax
on a college diploma was ten dollars, and
on an advertisement in a newspaper fifty cents.
In the same proportion every written contract
for the sale of property, every deed, every bill
of sale, bond, note, bill of exchange, or other
instrument used in business transactions, and
each separate paper used in legal proceedings
from the beginning of a suit to the end, had to
pay a stamp tax. An amusing but fair illustration of the effect of it was afforded when
Governor Tryon, on the 21st December, 1765,
submitted to the Council the question whether
he could issue writs of election for the new
Assembly on unstamped paper.

There was already the impost duty on all
the luxuries (including under this head such
articles as coffee and sugar); there was the tax
involved in the enforcement of the Navigation
Act, which, Bancroft says, "was the head-

spring that colored all the stream of American Independence," and these taxes were outside of the taxes imposed by the Colonial Legislatures for the purposes of local government.

So that, in the impoverished condition of the people, and amidst the trials and dangers that surrounded them, it looked like the very wantonness of tyranny to add a stamp tax to their burdens. It was, besides, as the Colonists and some of the wiser English statesmen insisted, an unconstitutional measure.

Daniel Dulaney, of Maryland, a lawyer whose ability in discussing the question profoundly impressed the public mind, both in England and America, and whose opinions were thought to have moulded those of Mr. Pitt, by whom they were publicly noticed with great honor, argued the rights of both parties with minute and elaborate learning, and his powerful reasoning strengthened the conviction of his countrymen that in opposing the act they were but vindicating their rights and defending their liberties. George Washington, in a letter to Francis Dandridge, in London, dated Mount Vernon, September 20th, 1765, says: "The Stamp Act imposed on the Colonies by the Parliament of Great Britain, engrosses the conversation of the speculative

part of the Colonists, who look upon this unconstitutional method of taxation as a direful
attack upon their liberties, and loudly exclaim
against the violation;" and he proceeds to
show that, merely as a revenue scheme, the act
and other ill-judged measures must prove dis-
astrous to Great Britain, inasmuch as they
would necessarily lessen importations into the
Colonies, and thereby hurt her manufacturers,
declaring at the same time that the Colonists
would dispense with all luxuries and live on
the necessaries which, he said, "are mostly to
be had within ourselves." He also declared
that the passage of the act would inevitably
close the Courts, as the Colonists could not
possibly comply with its provisions, and that
if such a result followed, the merchants of
Great Britain, trading to the Colonies, " would
not be among the last to wish for a repeal of
the act."* How much these merchants of
Great Britain were interested in the matter,
will appear from the following extract from
William Cullen Bryant's recently published
Popular History of the United States:†

" It is said that between 1765 and 1775, two-

*Washington's Letters, Vol. II, 343.
†Vol. III, 331.

thirds of the foreign commerce of Great Britain
was that which she conducted with America.
Between 1700 and 1760, the value of property
in England increased fifty per cent., and Pitt
declared this was wholly due to the American
Colonies. Speaking in 1766, he said, 'The
profit to Great Britain from the Colonies is
two millions a year. This is the fund that
carried you triumphantly through the last war.
You owe this to America.' Let it be remembered that Great Britain supplied three millions
of people in America with almost every manufactured article which they needed; that she
received from her Colonies the tobacco, and
much of the fish, indigo, rice, naval stores, and
other productions which she required; that
with her growing strength in the West Indies,
she used her Colonies on the main-land to feed
her islands, and it will be understood that
English merchants, and those who had to deal
with them in England, conceived high ideas of
the wealth to be derived from America."

It will, therefore, at once be seen from this
statement, which is amply verified by all the
authorities, that the Stamp Act was stupid and
suicidal legislation, which provoked resistance,
as well for commercial as for political reasons,
both in Great Britain and in the Colonies.
But the commercial reasons were the least powerful in the Colonies. It was the attempt to

subvert their liberties which, if submitted to, would only lead to further aggressions, that roused the Americans to fury and united them in a determination to resist the enforcement of the act with all their power and at every hazard; and, therefore, when certain intelligence of the final passage of it came, it produced a storm of angry opposition, and nowhere more than in North Carolina.

Tryon, in a letter to Conway, hereinafter given in full, says:

"In obedience to his Majesty's commands, communicated to me by the honor of your letter of the 12th of July last, it is with concern I acquaint you that the obstruction to the Stamp Act passed last session of Parliament, has been as general in this Province as in any Colony on the continent."

And in all his letters to the home government he reiterates the statement in the strongest language.

The first Assembly after Tryon's accession had met on the 3d of May at Wilmington, and it was immediately after their meeting, and before they had passed more than one or two acts, that intelligence of the passage of the Stamp Act by Parliament reached them. Tryon

knew what the popular sentiment was, and in
order to ascertain what would be the probable
action of the Assembly, he had an interview
with the Speaker, John Ashe, and asked him
the question.

Ashe's reply was, that the act "would be
resisted to blood and death." Thereupon
Tryon immediately issued a proclamation*
proroguing the Assembly to meet at Newbern
November 30th. He did not really intend,
however, that it should re-assemble at that
time unless the storm blew over; and afterwards, finding matters growing worse, he
issued another proclamation,† again proroguing
the Assembly until March 12th, assigning as
a reason that there appeared to be no immediate necessity for their meeting in November.
This proroguing of the Assembly on the 18th
May, and again October 25th, prevented the
election of delegates from North Carolina to
what is known in history as the Stamp Act
Congress—an explanation of the absence of
such delegates which does not seem to have
been known to the writers who have igno-
rantly criticised the State for a want of spirit

*May 18th, 1765.
†October 25th.

at that time. But, although the Assembly was thus prevented from meeting and giving expression to the public feeling, the people were not, and Colonel Hugh Waddell, though carrying the King's commission in his pocket, was one of the first to take the lead at Wilmington in denouncing the Act, and expressing a determination to resist it, in resolutions passed at public meetings held under the very nose of the Governor. These meetings were held in the summer of 1765, and were a part of the proceedings then going on in all the Colonies looking to the same end. But an event was soon to occur which—unknown to or ignored by some historians, and fixed at a wrong date by others—placed North Carolina at the head of the Colonies as offering the first *armed* resistance to the operation of the Stamp Act in America. In the other Colonies the feeling of resistance was as strong, and the demonstrations by the people were as earnest; but although flags were half-masted, effigies burned, processions formed, and stamp-masters forced to resign, *no open, armed resistance to an armed force occurred, except on the Cape Fear River.*

This occurrence took place when the sloop

of war *Diligence* arrived at Fort Johnston (now
Southport) at the mouth of the river with the
stamps. The arrival of the *Diligence* is, in all
the histories except Moore's, stated to have
occurred "in the first of the year," or "early
in the year" 1766—an error arising from the
fact that Tryon's proclamation announcing
her arrival was dated January 6th of that year.
Moore's history places her arrival on the 28th
September, 1765. The true date was November 28th, 1765.

On the 16th day of November,[*] the people,
under the lead of Colonel John Ashe and
others, went to Tryon's house and demanded
William Houston (not James Houston, as
invariably stated in every published account
of the affair), who had been appointed stamp-
master, and upon Tryon's refusal to surrender
him they made preparations to burn the house.
Tryon then requested Colonel Ashe to step in
and talk with the stamp-master, which he did,
and Houston, realizing his danger if he refused
the demand made upon him to resign his office,
agreed to accompany Colonel Ashe to the
street, and, escorted thence by a large crowd,
they went to the Court-House and there, in

---

[*]Tryon's letter to Hon. Seymour Conway, Feb. 29, 1766.

the presence of the Mayor and public officers, Houston took and subscribed the following oath:

"I do hereby promise that I never will receive any stamp-paper which may arrive from Europe, in consequence of any act lately passed in the Parliament of Great Britain, nor officiate in any manner as stamp-master in the distribution of stamps within the Province of North Carolina, either directly or indirectly. I do hereby notify all the inhabitants of His Majesty's Province of North Carolina, that notwithstanding my having received information of my being appointed to said office of stamp-master, I will not apply hereafter for any stamp-paper, or to distribute the same until such time as it shall be agreeable to the inhabitants of this Province.

"Hereby declaring that I do execute these presents of my own free will and accord, without any equivocation or mental reservation whatever.

"In witness hereof, I have hereunto set my hand this 16th November, 1765.

"WILLIAM HOUSTON."*

Upon the taking and signing the oath by Houston, the crowd gave three cheers and then dispersed.

---

*Tryon's dispatch, Dec. 26th.

Twelve days afterward the *Diligence* arrived in the Cape Fear river with the stamps, and the welcome which awaited her captain must have astonished him. His name was Phipps, and his vessel was a twenty-gun sloop of war, which was cruising off the coast of Virginia and the Carolinas. He brought the stamps from Virginia, whither they had been sent from England, and, doubtless, anticipated no trouble whatever in delivering them to the Collector of the port of Brunswick. The idea of resistance of any kind probably never occurred to him, and a suggestion of armed defiance on the part of the people on shore would have seemed the wildest absurdity to a commander of one of His Majesty's war-ships.

Comfortably pacing his deck as the gallant sloop, with colors flying and all her canvass set, glided curtseying across the bar like a fine lady entering a drawing-room, the Captain was doubtless already enjoying in anticipation the sideboard and table refreshments that awaited him in the hospitable mansions of the Cape Fear planters, and eager to stand, gun in hand, by one of the tall pines of Brunswick and watch the coming of the antlered monarch of the forest before the inspiring music of the hounds.

As the *Diligence* bowls along "with a bone in her mouth" across the ruffled bosom of the beautiful bay into which the river expands opposite Fort Johnston, a puff of white smoke leaps from her port quarter followed by a roar of salutation from one of her guns; an answering thunder of welcome comes from the fort, and the proud ship walks the waters towards the town of Brunswick, eight miles farther up the river towards Wilmington. An hour later she sights the town, and a little while afterwards, with a graceful sweep and a rushing keel, she gradually puts her nose in the wind as if scenting trouble; and then, at the shrill sound of the boatswain's whistle, the growling chains release the anchor from its long sus-. pense, and the *Diligence* rests opposite to the Custom House of Brunswick, with her grinning port-holes open and all her guns exposed. Then her rigging blocks chuckle as she lowers and clews her sails, and she rides at her moorings beneath the flag of the Mistress of the Seas.

The Captain at once observes that the little town seems to be unusually lively and expectant. He soon discovers the cause. A considerable body of armed men occupy the streets and line the shore. Presently he is informed

that Colonel Hugh Waddell, an experienced
soldier, who had been on the lookout for the
Diligence with the militia of Brunswick County,
had notified Colonel Ashe of New Hanover of
his movements, and these two gentlemen, with
the armed militia of both counties, confronted
him and informed him that they would resist
the landing of the stamps and would fire on
any one attempting it.

Here was one of His Majesty's twenty-gun
sloops of war openly defied and threatened by
British subjects armed and drawn up in battle
array! Here was treason, open, flagrant and
in the broad light of day—treason, armed and
led by the most distinguished soldier of the
Province and the Speaker of the Assembly!

The Captain of the *Diligence* prudently concluded that it would be folly to attempt to land
the stamps in the face of such a threat, backed
by such force, and promised a compliance with
the demands of the people. The "Sons of
Liberty," as they were afterwards called, then
seized one of the boats of the *Diligence*, and
leaving a guard at Brunswick marched with
it mounted on a cart to Wilmington, where
there was a triumphal procession through the
streets, and at night a general illumination of
the town.

"And this," said an eloquent North Carolinian, "was more than ten years before the Declaration of Independence, and more than nine before the battle of Lexington, and nearly eight years before the Boston 'Tea Party.' The destruction of the tea was done in the night by men in disguise. And history blazons it, and New England boasts of it, and the fame of it is world-wide. But this other act, more gallant and daring, done in open day by well-known men, with arms in their hands, and under the King's flag—who remembers, or who tells of it."[*]

Contemplating this act, and many other kindred ones done by her sons, well did the orator ask, "When will history do justice to North Carolina?"

It being the duty of Governor Tryon, as a matter of course, to report all this business to the home government, he determined to say nothing about the armed resistance to the *Diligence*, but to report only the facts in regard to the compulsion of the Stamp-Master to resign, and to explain the failure to land the stamps by the assertion that, as there was no

[*]Hon. George Davis, Address at the University of N. C., June, 1855.

one to distribute them, *he* directed them to be
kept on board that vessel. The humiliation
to which he had been subjected in his own
house in which Houston had taken refuge (of
which fact he likewise avoided all mention),
was sufficiently galling, without adding an
account of it, or of the armed defiance of one
of His Majesty's men-of-war by the same people. Besides, as appears from his conduct and
his dispatch to Conway, he was anxious to
smooth over the trouble and conciliate the
people, whose good will he desired to cultivate,
whose condition he knew to be depressed, and
whose spirit he was obliged to respect. Indeed,
the whole tone of the dispatch was deprecatory
and regretful, and justifies the suspicion that
Tryon sympathized with those who regarded
the Stamp Act as most unwise and oppressive
legislation, although his position was such as
to prevent him from openly saying so. This
dispatch which, like the others in his letter-
book, has never been published up to the time
when these pages are written, is here given in
full, so far as it relates to the event above
described.

BRUNSWICK 26 Decr 1765.

" *The Right Hon'ble H'y Seymour Conway*

In obedience to His Majesty's commands communicated to me by the honor of your letter of the 12th of July last, it is with concern I acquaint you that the obstruction to the Stamp Act passed last session of Parliament has been as general in this province as in any Colony on the continent, tho' their irregular proceedings have been attended with no mischief, or are by any means formidable. I am much of the opinion that whatever measures are prescribed and enforced by his Majesty's authority to the more formidable Colonies to the Northward will meet with a ready acquiesence in the Southern provinces, without the necessity of any military force. The first intelligence of the general alarm which was spread against the Stamp Act in this Colony was in October last, at a time I lay extremely ill of the fevers of this country, which with repeated relapses I have experienced these five months past. I was very impatient to seize the first opportunity to communicate my sentiments to the merchants of New Hanover and Brunswick Counties, who are the persons that carry on the commerce of Cape Fear River (and where I imagined the stamps would arrive) on the then situation of public affairs. On the 18th November near fifty of the above gentlemen waited on me to dinner when I urged to them the expediency of permitting the circulation of the stamps, but as my health at that time would not allow me to write down any speech I must beg leave to refer you, Sir, to the enclosed Carolina Gazette of the 27th Novr in which you will find nearly the substance of what I declared and proposed to the above gentlemen. Their answer and my reply are inclosed.

Two days before the above meeting, Mr. Houston the Distributor of the stamps was compelled in the Court House in Wilmington and in the presence of the Mayor and some Aldermen to resign his office. The stamps arrived the 28th of November last in his Majesty's Sloop, the *Diligence* Capt Phipps commander, but as there was no Distributor or other officer of the stamps in this country after Mr. Houston's resignation the stamps still remain on board the said ship. No vessels have been cleared out since the first of November from this river or from any other in this province that I have received intelligence of. Some merchants from Wilmington applied to me for certificates for their ships, specifying that no stamps were to be had, which I declined granting, referring them to the officers of his Majesty's Customs. They have been as assiduous in obstructing the reception of the stamps as any of the inhabitants.

No business is transacted in the Courts of Judicature, tho' the Courts have been regularly opened and all civil government is now at a stand. This stagnation of all public business and commerce under the low circumstances of the inhabitants must be attended with fatal consequences to this colony, if it subsists but for a few months longer. There is little or no specie circulating in the maritime Counties of this province, and what is in circulation in the back Counties is so very inconsiderable that the Attorney General assures me that the stamp duties on the instruments used in the five Superior Courts of this province would in one year require all the specie in the country; the business which is likewise transacted in the twenty nine inferior, or County Courts, the many instruments which pass through the Sheriffs' hands and other civil officers; those in the Land Office, and many other instruments used in transactions of public business were the reasons which induced me to believe the operation in all its parts impracticable, and which likewise prompted me to make my proposals for the ease and convenience of the People, and to endeavor to reconcile them to this Act of Parliament.

On the 20th of last month I opened and proclaimed my commission at Wilmington, when I consulted his Majesty's Council if any measures could be proposed to induce the people to receive the stamps. They were unanimously of opinion that nothing further could be done than what I have already offered.

I have his Majesty's writs for a new election of Assembly, but shall not meet them till next April at Newbern— *   *   *   *

I am, Sir &c

WM TRYON"

Not long after this event, and in pursuance of the same purpose of resisting the Stamp Act in every way—even to the point of arresting and punishing the Captain of a war-vessel himself, if necessary—another very lively incident occurred on the Cape Fear which astonished and infuriated Tryon and his friends, and added greatly to his already sore humiliation; but it was no more than might have been expected, after the resistance to the landing of the stamps and the previous exaction of the oath from Houston on the 16th November.

Early in February, and while the men-of-war *Viper* and *Diligence* were still lying in the river off Brunswick, two merchant vessels, the *Dobbs* and the *Patience*, the one from St. Christophers and the other from Philadelphia, arrived. The Collector of the port, Colonel Wm. Dry, upon examining their clearance papers, ascertained that there were no stamps attached to them, as required by the provisions of the Stamp Act, and, as was doubtless his duty, he took the papers and reported the facts to the Captain of the *Viper*, Captain Jacob Lobb. Captain Lobb immediately seized the vessels, regardless of the assurances of their Captains that it was impossible for them to comply with the law, for the reason that when they left Philadelphia and St. Christophers no stamps could be obtained. As soon as it became known that these vessels had been seized under such circumstances there was great excitement, and the news spread with such rapidity that very soon five hundred and eighty armed men, besides one hundred without arms, were assembled and Colonel Hugh Waddell was chosen as their commander.

What followed is told in detail by Governor Tryon in his dispatches to the home government, and, as this narrative has never been published, it is here given, as taken from his letter-book now in the Executive Department at Raleigh. There are some facts which were suppressed by Tryon in this narrative, just as he suppressed all mention of the resistance to the landing of the stamps on the 28th November, supplying the omission with the general statement that as Houston had resigned, "the stamps still remain on board the said ship;" but as the omissions in his account of the affair are not important, the narrative is given as he wrote it, as follows:

The Right Honorable Henry Seymour Conway, Esq., one of his Majesty's Principal Secretaries of State:

BRUNSWICK, the 25th February, 1766.

SIR, As I wish to give you as particular a relation for his Majesty's information as I possibly can of an illegal assembly of men in arms, assembled at Brunswick on the 19th inst. I have collected all the letter correspondence that has come to my knowledge, previous to the 19th inst. during the time the men remained in arms, as well as after they dispersed.

In this letter I shall chiefly confine myself to the narrations of the actions and conduct of the body assembled, desiring leave to refer you to the letters as they occur in point of order, and time.

The Seizures Capt. Lobb made of the Dobbs and Patience sloops, (as by his letter to the collector for taking the papers and the Attorney General's opinion taken thereon) was an affair I did not interfere with; In the first instance I never was applied to, and in the second, I thought it rested with Capt. Lobb.

On the 16th in the evening Mr. Dry, the Collector, waited on me with a letter he received dated from Wilmington the 15th of February 1766 and at the same time informed me he had sent the subscribers word he should wait on them the next day. I strongly recommended him to put the papers belonging to the Patience Sloop on board the Viper (those of the Dobbs

had some time before been given up to the
owner on his delivering security for them) as
I apprehended, I said, those very subscribers
would compel him to give them up; His answer
was "They might take them from him but he
would never give them up without Capt. Lobb's
order." The weather on the 17th prevented
Mr. Dry from going to Wilmington till the
next day.

The next intelligence I received was in the
dusk of the evening of the 19th soon after 6
o'clock by letter delivered me by Mr. George
Moore and Mr. Cornelius Harnett bearing date
the 19th and signed "John Ashe, Thomas
Lloyd, Alexander Lillington." My letter of
the same night directed "to the Commanding
Officer either of the Viper or Diligence Sloops
of War" will explain the opinion I entertained
of the offer made of a guard of gentlemen, and
my declaration to the detachment I found sur-
rounding my house. This letter my servant
about three in the morning put on board the
Diligence who lay moored opposite to my house
at the distance of four or five hundred yards,
and returned to me again in a short space of
time with Capt. Phipps letter in answer. Soon
after I had put up the lights required Capt.
Phipps came himself on shore to me, the guards
having quitted the posts they had taken round
the house, and on the beach : With a most
generous warmth and zeal Capt. Phipps offered
me every service his ship or himself could
afford. I assured him the services I wished to

receive from his Majesty's sloops consisted
wholly in the protection of the Fort. That as
Capt. Dalrymple had but five men in garrison
to defend eight eighteen pounders, eight nine
pounders, and twenty three swivel guns all
mounted and fit for service together with a
considerable quantity of ammunition, I wrote an
order to Capt. Dalrymple " to obey all orders
he might receive from the Commanding Officer
either of the Viper or Diligence sloops of war,"
and desired Capt. Phipps would send it to the
Fort. I made it so general because Capt.
Phipps told me neither of the Sloops had a
pilot then on board, and that it was uncertain
which ship could first get down to the Fort
distant four leagues from where the ships then
lay off Brunswick; Capt. Phipps after a stay
on shore of about ten minutes returned on
board the Diligence.

On the 20th about 12 o'clock at noon Capt.
Lobb sent to desire I would meet him on board
the Diligence, which request I immediately
complied with and at the same time the Collector Mr. Dry came on board. There were
then present, the Captains Lobb and Phipps,
Mr. McGwire, Vice Judge of the Admiralty,
the Collector, and myself. Capt. Lobb told me
he had had a committee from the inhabitants
in arms on board his ship, that they demanded
the possession of the sloops he had seized and
that he was to give them his answer in the
afternoon. Mr. Dry the Collector informed me
that his desk was broke open on the 19th in

the evening and the unstampt papers belonging to the Patience and Ruby sloops forcibly
taken from him. He said he knew most of
the persons that came into his house at that
time but he did not see who broke open the
desk and took out the papers. Capt. Lobb
seemed not satisfied with the legality of his
seizure of the Ruby sloop (seized subsequent
to the papers that were sent to the Attorney
General for his opinion, on the Dobbs and
Patience) and declared he would return her to
the master or owner; but that he would insist
on the papers belonging to the Patience being
returned, which were taken from the Collectors
desk, and that he would not give up the Sloop
Patience. I approved of these resolutions and
desired that he would not in the conduct of
this affair consider my family, myself or my
property, that I was greatly solicitous for the
honor of government and his Majesty's interest
in the present exigency, and particularly
recommended to him the protection of Fort
Johnston. I then returned on shore. In the
evening Capt Phipps waited on me from on
board the Viper, and acquainted me that all
was settled; that Capt Lobb had given his
consent for the owners to take possession of
the Sloops Ruby and Patience, as the copy of
Capt Lobbs orders for that purpose will declare.
This report was not consistent with the
determinations I concluded Capt Lobb left the
Diligence in, when I met him according to his
appointment but a few hours before.

To be regular in point of time I must now
speak of some further conduct of the inhabitants in arms, who were continually coming
into Brunswick from different counties. This
same evening of the 20th inst. Mr. Pennington, his Majesty's Comptroller came to let me
know there had been a search after him, and
as he guessed they wanted him to do some act
that would be inconsistent with the duty of his
office, he came to acquaint me with this enquiry
and search. I told him I had a bed at his service, and desired he would remain with me.
The next morning the 21st about eight o'clock,
I saw Mr. Pennington going from my house
with Col James Moore. I called him back,
and as Col Moore returned with him I desired
to know if he had any business with Mr. Pennington. He said the gentlemen assembled
wanted to speak with him. I desired Col.
Moore would inform the gentlemen, Mr. Pennington, his Majesty's Comptroller, I had
occasion to employ on dispatches for his
Majesty's service, therefore could not part with
him. Col Moore then went away and in five
minutes afterwards I found the avenues to my
house again shut up by different parties of
armed men. Soon after the following note was
sent and the answer annexed returned:

"SIR
 "The Gentlemen assembled for the redress
"of grievances desirous of seeing Mr. Pen-
"nington to speak with him sent Col Moore
"to desire his attendance, and understand that

"he was stayed by your Excellency, they
"therefore request that your Excellency will
"be pleased to let him attend, otherwise it will
"not be in the power of the Directors appointed,
"to prevent the ill consequences that may
"attend a refusal.   They don't intend the least
"injury to Mr. Pennington."
   Friday the 21st February 1766.
   To His Excellency.

THE ANSWER.

   "Mr Pennington being employed by his
"Excellency on dispatches for his Majesty's
"service, any gentleman that may have busi-
"ness with him may see him at the Governor's
"house."
   21st February 1766

   It was about 10 o'clock when I observed a body
of men in arms, from four to five hundred, move
towards the house.   A detachment of sixty
men came down the avenue, and the main body
drew up in front, in sight, and within three
hundred yards of the house.   Mr. Harnett, a
representative in the Assembly for Wilmington, came at the head of the detachment, and
sent a message to speak with Mr Pennington.
When he came into the house he told Mr.
Pennington the gentlemen wanted him.   I
answered, Mr. Pennington came into my house
for refuge, he was a Crown Officer, and as such
I would give him all the protection my roof,

and the dignity of the character I held in this
province, could afford him. Mr. Harnett hoped
I would let him go, as the people were determined to take him out of the house if he should
be longer detained; an insult he said they
wished to avoid offering to me: An insult, I
replied, that would not tend to any great consequence, after they had already offered every
insult they could offer, by investing my house,
and making me in effect a prisoner before any
grievance, or oppression, had been first represented to me. Mr. Pennington grew very
uneasy, said he would choose to go to the gentlemen; I again repeated my offers of protection, if he chose to stay. He declared, and
desired I would remember, that whatever oaths
might be imposed on him, he should consider
them as acts of compulsion and not of free will;
and further added that he would rather resign
his office than do any act contrary to his duty.
If that was his determination, I told him, he
had better resign before he left me. Mr.
Harnett interposed, with saying he hoped he
would not do that: I enforced the recommendation for resignation. He consented, paper
was brought, and his resignation executed, and
received. I then said, Mr. Pennington, now
sir, you may go; Mr. Harnett went out with
him; the detachment retired to the town. Mr.
Pennington afterwards informed me, they got
him in the midst of them when Mr. Ward,
master of the Patience, asked him to enter his
sloop. Mr. Pennington assured him he could

not, as he had resigned his office. He was
afterwards obliged to take an oath that he
would never issue any stamped paper in this
province. The above oath the Collector
informed me he was obliged to take, as were
all the clerks of the County Courts, and other
public officers. The inhabitants, having re-
dressed after the manner described their grievances complained of, left the town of Brunswick
about 1 o'clock on the 21st. In the evening I
went on board the Viper and acquainted Capt
Lobb I apprehended the conditions he had
determined to abide by when I left the Diligence, were different to the concessions he had
made to the committee appointed for the redress
of grievances: That I left the Diligence in the
full persuasion he was to demand a restitution
of the papers or clearances of the Patience
sloop, and not to give up the possession of that
vessel: That I found he had given up the
sloop Patience, and himself not in possession
of the papers. He answered "As to the papers,
"he had attested copies of them, and as to
"the sloop, he had done no more than what
"he had offered before this disturbance hap-
"pened at Brunswick." I could not help
owning I thought the detaining the Patience
became a point that concerned the honor of
government, and that I found my situation
very unpleasant, as most of the people by
going up to Wilmington in the sloops would
remain satisfied and report thro' the province,
they had obtained every point they came to

redress, while at the same time I had the mor-
tification to be informed his Majesty's ordnance
at Fort Johnston was spiked. This is the substance of what passed on board the Viper. On
the 22d Capt. Phipps accompanied me to Fort
Johnston, where I found Capt Dalrymple sick
in bed, two men only in garrison, and all the
cannon that were mounted, spiked with nails.
I gave orders for the nails to be immediately
drilled out, which will be executed without
prejudice to the pieces. I returned to Brunswick in the evening, and the next morning sent
my letter bearing date the 23d to Capt. Lobb
to desire his reasons for spiking the cannon
&c. He returned me his reasons for this conduct by letter the 24th inst.

Capt Lobb's complaint relative to the provisions for his Majesty's sloops being stopt at
Wilmington with the contractor's certificate of
the manner of this restraint and my letter to
the Mayor of Wilmington to require his assistance in furnishing the provision demanded, will
be fully, I hope, understood by that correspondence.

By the best accounts I have received the
number of this insurrection amounted to 580
men in arms, and upwards of 100 unarmed.
The Mayor and Corporation of Wilmington
and most all of the gentlemen and planters of
the counties of Brunswick, New Hanover,
Duplin, and Bladen, with some masters of
vessels, composed this corps. I am informed
and believe the majority of this association

were either compelled into this service or were ignorant what their grievances were. I except the principals. I have enclosed a copy of the association formed to oppose the Stamp Act.

Thus, Sir, I have endeavored to lay before you the first springs of this disturbance as well as the particular conduct of the parties concerned in it; and I have done this as much as I possibly could without prejudice, or passion, favor or affection. I should be extremely glad if you, Sir, could honor me with his Majesty's commands in the present exigency of affairs in this colony and in the mean time will study to conduct myself with the assistance of his Majesty's Council in such manner as will best secure the safety and honor of government and the peace of the inhabitants of this province.

I am, Sir, with all possible respect and esteem.

Copies of Letters and papers referred to in the preceding letter :

(COPY.)

VIPER, CAPE FEAR, 14th January, 1766.

SIR,

As the Sloops Dobbs and Patience not having their clearances on stampt paper according to act of Parliament I have detained them, and herewith you will receive the papers in order to their being prosecuted in the Court of Ad-

8

miralty as I am directed by the commissioners of the Customs, I am Sir,

Your humble servant,

JACOB LOBB.

William Dry, Esq.

———

(COPY.)

CUSTOM HOUSE, PORT BRUNSWICK,
16th January 1766.

DEAR SIR,

By instruction from the Surveyor General, I am ordered in case any of the Men of War should make any seizures to receive the cause of seizure and her papers from them and to transmit them to you for your opinion which I am to be ruled by whether to prosecute or not.

This therefore serves to enclose you the papers of two vessels, one from Philadelphia the other from St. Christophers which Capt. Lobb hath seized for not having Stampt Papers as you'll see by his letter to me here enclosed. The papers are in separate packets, the one parcell are copies of the originals and the others are the original papers which Mr. Quince desired I might send as belonging to his vessel; all which I must entreat the favor of you to look over and to return me your opinion by this express which I send on purpose. I beg the messenger may be dispatched.

I am Dear Sir,

Your most obedient servant,

WILLIAM DRY.

Robert Jones Jun. Esq.

(COPY.)

OCCANECHY 3d February 1766.

DEAR SIR,

I received yours of the 16th ult. pr. your messenger, & have perused the papers sent therewith, from whence I have made a state of the case you desire to be advised about, as it occurs to me, and subjoined to it my opinion in full, both which you will receive enclosed. As matters are circumstanced I think you ought to proceed in prosecuting both vessels, lest your neglect should be deemed a connivance at the opposition made to the Stamp Act, which in an officer of the Crown probably may be thought worthy of censure.

Pray let Mr. Quince have a sight of the Case and my opinion, as by my letter to him I have referred him to you for that purpose.

I was from home when the messenger came and did not return till last night which occasioned his tarrying.

I am,
    Dear Sir,
Your most obedt & very hum: servant
       ROBERT JONES, JUN.

P. S. The Act does not require that Registers should be on Stampt paper.

To the Honble William Dry, Esq.

———

(COPY.)

State of the case relative to the Sloops Dobbs and Patience, lately arrived in Cape Fear River, the one from Philadelphia, the other from St. Christophers.

It is supposed that no Stampt Paper could be procured by the Officers of the Customs in the ports from whence the said vessels sailed, therefore the Captains obtained clearances, certificates, &c. on common paper and proceeded to Cape Fear, where they are seized by Capt Lobb, Commander of His Majesty's Sloop Viper, who makes information to the Collector of the Port, requiring him to commence prosecutions against them.

Quere 1. Is failing to obtain Clearances &c. on stampt paper a proper cause for seizing the said vessels and to be considered as a neglect of the duties required by the Acts of Trade sufficient to induce a Court of Admiralty to decree vessels and cargoes forfeited?

2. Upon proof being made that it was impossible to obtain Clearances &c on Stampt Paper of the officers of the customs in the ports from whence the said vessels sailed, will it not be a sufficient cause to induce the Court to decree in favor of the owners of the said vessels?

3. If it is necessary to prosecute on Capt Lobbs information, must the prosecution be commenced in the Court of Admiralty at Cape Fear, or must the said vessels be sent to Halifax in order to be libelled?

In answer to the first question.—The Clearances &c being on common paper it is the same as if these vessels had sailed without clearances, and of course they are liable to be seized, and

I think condemned by a Court of Admiralty with their cargoes.

2d. Reason does not require impossibilities and Courts of Admiralty often decree favorably on the part of the owners of vessels and cargoes where it does not appear that any fraud was intended to the crown; especially where all has been done that it was in the power of the Captains or owners of vessels to do; but the Captains of these vessels seem to me to have been guilty of great neglect. They should have tendered the Kings duties to the officers of the customs and demanded proper clearances &c. and on being refused they should have made the like tender to a Notary Public and offered a protest. Had these matters been complied with so as to be duly proved on a tryal, I should think the Judge would decree that the vessels and cargoes were not forfeited.

3. If prosecutions are intended against these vessels, they must be sent to Halifax, for should they be libelled here, and the proceedings carried on upon common paper, such proceedings will be mere nullities and not alter the property either of the vessels or cargoes. As to the provision in the Stamp Act that penalties should be sued for where offences against that act are committed, that must be understood of pecuniary penalties specified in the said Act, and can have no relation to matters mentioned in the above case. Upon the whole

it is my opinion that it is the duty of the Collector to prosecute on the informations received.
ROBERT JONES JUN.

———

(COPY.)

19th February 1766.

SIR,

The Inhabitants dissatisfied with the particular restrictions laid on the trade of this river only, have determined to march to Brunswick in hopes of obtaining in a peaceable manner, a redress of their grievances from the Commanding Officer of his Majesty's ships, and have compelled us to conduct them; We therefore think it our duty to acquaint your Excellency, that we are fully determined to protect from insult your person and property, and that if it will be agreeable to your Excellency, a guard of gentlemen shall be immediately detached for that purpose.

We have the honor to be with the greatest respect

      Sir,

Your Excellency's most obedient

      Humble servants,

        JOHN ASHE,

        THOS. LOYD,

        ALEX. LILLINGTON.

To His Excellency William Tryon, Esq.

BRUNSWICK 19th February 1766.
Eleven at Night

SIR,

Between the hours of six and seven o'clock this evening, Mr. George Moore and Mr. Cornelius Harnett waited on me at my house, and delivered to me a letter signed by three gentlemen. The inclosed is a copy from the original. I told Mr. Moore and Mr. Harnett, that as I had no fears or apprehensions for my person or property, I wanted no guard, therefore desired the gentlemen might not come to give their protection where it was not necessary or required, and that I would send the gentlemen an answer in writing tomorrow morning. Mr. Moore and Mr. Harnett might stay about five or six minutes in my house, Instantly after their leaving me, I found my house surrounded with armed men to the number I estimate at one hundred and fifty. I had some altercation with some of the gentlemen who informed me their business was to see Capt Lobb whom they were informed was at my house; Capt Paine then desired me to give my word and honor whether Capt Lobb was in my house or not. I positively refused to make any such declaration, but as they had force in their hands I said they might brake open my locks and force my doors. This they declared they had no intention of doing; just after this and other discourse they got intelligence that Capt Lobb was not in my

house.   The majority of the men in arms then
went towards the town of Brunswick and left
a number of men to watch the avenues of my
house, therefore think it doubtful if I can get
this letter safely conveyed.

I esteem it my duty, Sir, to inform you as
Fort Johnston has but one officer, and five men
in garrison, the Fort will stand in need of all
the assistance the Viper and Diligence Sloops
can give the Commanding Officer there, should
any insult be offered to his Majesty's fort or
stores, in which case it is my duty to request
of you to repel force with force; and to take
on board his Majesty's sloops so much of his
Majesty's ordnance, stores and ammunition,
out of the said fort as you shall think necessary for the benefit of the service.

I am Sir,

Your most humble servant,

(Signed)   Wm. Tryon.

To the Commanding Officer either of the Viper
or Diligence Sloops of War.

———

(copy.)

Sir,

I have received your Excellency's favor and
am much concerned at the uneasiness this
accident will have given you. I have been
disappointed in two attempts to see your Excellency to-night, one very early tother late.
I had immediately, upon hearing two hundred
men were gone down, sent Lieut Calder with
five men and spikes for the guns if Capt Dalrymple thought them necessary, and to give

him any other assistance that was necessary.
I believe they were down in time. I hope if
this gets safe your Excellency will let me
know it by showing a light in each of the
middle windows above stairs. If I see that
signal I will inform your Excellency of the
success of my boat by hauling down the pen-
dant at sunrise or soon after. Capt Lobb
received a deputation to desire he would come
on shore, which he refused.

    I am, your Excellency's most obedient
        And most humble servant,
                C. J. PHIPPS.
To His Excellency Governor Tryon, &c. &c.

(COPY.)

SIR,
    You will obey all orders you may receive
either from the Commanding Officer of the
Viper or Diligence sloops of war.
    I am
        Your very humble servant,
           (Signed)   WM. TRYON.
19 February 1776.
To Capt. Dalrymple.

(COPY.)

VIPER SLOOP, CAPE FEAR,
          20 February 1766.

SIR,
    Not thinking it proper to detain the Sloop
Ruby any longer, desire you will deliver her

to the proper master, Mr. Horner, for which
this shall be a sufficient warrant.

I am Sir,
Your most humble servant,
JACOB LOBB.

To William Dry, Esq.
Collector for Brunswick.

(COPY.)

VIPER SLOOP, CAPE FEAR,
20 Feb'y 1766.

SIR,
As there is perishable commodities on board
the Sloop Patience, detained by me, you may,
if you think it consistent with your duty,
deliver up the same with the Vessel and cargoe
upon sufficient security for them.

I am Sir,
Your very humble servant,
JACOB LOBB.

To William Dry, Esq.
Collector at Brunswick.

(COPY.)

BRUNSWICK, 23d February 1766.

SIR,
I was yesterday with Capt. Phipps at Fort
Johnston where I found twenty three swivel
guns, eight eighteen pounders and eight nine
pounders spiked. I demanded of Capt. Dalrymple, the Commanding Officer, his authority
for spiking the cannon. He produced your
order and said Lieut. Calder of the Diligence,

in consequence of it, spiked the above cannon.
As I understand your midshipman was yesterday disappointed in getting copies of my
instructions to Capt. Dalrymple, and your
order to him, I insert them both, Vidt.

SIR,
 "You will obey all orders you may receive
"either from the Commanding Officer of the
"Viper or Diligence Sloops of War."
   I am, &c.
      WM. TRYON.

19 February 1766.
 To Capt. Dalrymple.

 "I think its necessary at this time, you will
"render the guns at Fort Johnston unservice-
"able, as there is a number of men which
"intend insulting his Majesty's ships in this
"river. I am
   "Your humble Servant,
     "JACOB LOBB."

I must observe that the reason you gave in
this order, is totally contrary to every sentiment I entertained, as I hope my letter of the
19th, delivered to you by Lieut. Calder will
justify, directed to the Commanding Officer
either of the Viper or Diligence Sloops of War,
as well as my conversation on board the Diligence on the 20th where you desired I would
meet you. I never had a suspicion that it was
in the power of the persons assembled in arms
to insult his Majesty's ships in this river. The
object of my consideration was the protection

of the fort. I therefore wish to receive from you the reasons why you thought the spiking of the guns a necessary step to prevent his Majesty's ships from being insulted, or what other motives you had for ordering the guns to be spiked. This request I make that I may be furnished with the proper causes for such a proceeding, in order to transmit them to his Majesty's Principal Secretary of State with my other dispatches.

I am, &c. Sir,
Your most humble servant,
(Signed) WM. TRYON.
To Capt. Lobb.

——

(COPY.)

VIPER SLOOP, BRUNSWICK,
The 24th Feb'ry, 1766.

SIR,
I received your Excellency's Letter of the 23d inst. desiring me to give your Excellency my reasons for ordering the guns at Fort Johnston to be spiked. Pursuant to your Excellency's letter of the 19th inst. signifying to me that as Fort Johnston had but one officer and five men in garrison and of its standing in need of all the assistance the Viper and Diligence could give the commanding officer there, should any insult be offered to his Majesty's fort, or stores, and likewise your Excellency's request to repel force with force, I, on information the same evening from Lieut. Calder, corroborated by that of several other

gentlemen, that a party of men, consisting of three or four hundred, under the command of Col. Waddell, were on their march to Fort Johnston in order to take possession of it, as there was no possibility of getting the ships down, being night and no pilots to be had early enough to prevent their making their quarters good, sent Lieut. Calder in a boat with your Excellency's order addrest to Capt. Dalrymple commanding that he should comply with any orders he should receive from myself or Capt. Phipps, with one from me to render the cannon unserviceable by spiking them up, to the end of facilitating our repossession as soon as the ships could arrive before it.

I am with respect,
Your Excellency's most obedient
Humble Servant,
JACOB LOBB.
To His Excellency Governor Tryon.

While this was going on the people in Wilmington were not idle. They seized the boat of the contractor for supplies to the men-of-war, and the consequence was that the crews of the *Viper* and *Diligence*, finding themselves with only one day's rations of bread, and the only possible source of supply thus cut off, were in a fair way to starve. This compelled Tryon to terms, and the Solicitor of the Court of Admiralty, Robert Jones, Esq., made a virtue of necessity, and accepted the explanation of the captains of the two merchant vessels in regard to the impossibility of procuring stamps, and released their vessels. The correspondence in relation to the seizure of the boat, as, found in Tryon's dispatches, is as follows:

(COPY.)

VIPER·SLOOP, CAPE FEAR,
22d February 1766.
SIR,

I beg leave to acquaint your Excellency that by my order of the 5th inst. there was a demand for provisions given to the Contractor's Agent, Mr. William Dry, for the use of the complement of men on board his Majesty's Sloop under my command, which demand is not complied with, and I find by a certificate from Mr. Dry the provisions were denied being brought to his Majesty's Sloop by the Inhabitants of Wilmington. I must beg leave to acquaint your Excellency that there is no more bread on board than to serve the Sloop's company tomorrow, and do request your Excellency's advice. Inclosed your Excellency will receive a copy of Mr. Dry's certificate. I am with respect,
Your Excellency's
Obedient humble servant,
JACOB LOBB.
To His Excellency Governor Tryon.

(COPY.)

These are to certify that there was a demand made to me by Capt. Jacob Lobb of his Majesty's Sloop Viper for a supply of provisions for the said Sloop on the Fifth inst. and that there was a boat and hands sent by me to Wilmington for the same, that the men belonging to the boat were taken up and put into gaol, that the inhabitants and people of the province would not suffer any provisions to be shipt on board the boat for the use of his Majesty's sloop.

Dated at Brunswick, 21 February 1766.

WM. DRY.

———

(COPY.)

BRUNSWICK the 22d February 1766.

SIR,

In answer to your letter I can only observe that as you have thought it expedient to redress the grievances which were the pretended causes of the town of Wilmington's withholding the necessary provisions for his Majesty's Sloops, I should imagine the contractor's agent would meet with no obstruction at present in obtaining the necessary supply. If the provisions are not brought to the Viper tomorrow I desire you will inform me by a line.

I am, &c.

WM. TRYON.

To Capt. Lobb.

(COPY.)

VIPER SLOOP, BRUNSWICK,
24 Feb'y, 1766.

SIR,

I received your Excellency's letter of the
22d inst. signifying to me your Excellency's
desire of being acquainted if the provisions did
not arrive the 23d, and in return beg leave to
acquaint your Excellency they are not yet
arrived.   I am with respect,
      Your Excellency's
      Most obedient humble servant,
                              JACOB LOBB.
To His Excellency Governor Tryon.

———

(COPY.)

BRUNSWICK the 24 February 1766.
MR. MAYOR.

Capt. Lobb having lodged a complaint with
me, dated the 22d inst. that the Contractor's
boat, with provisions for the use of his Majesty's
ships was detained at Wilmington and the
boatmen put into gaol by the inhabitants of
that town, I desire to know the proper causes
for such conduct that I may transmit them to
his Majesty.   The Viper sloop is at present
without bread.   I do therefore require your
assistance that the contractor may be furnished
with the necessary provisions as soon as possible.
      I am Sir, &c.
                              WM. TRYON.
Moses John De Rosset, Esq.

(COPY.)

WILMINGTON 28 February 1766.

SIR,

Your Excellency's letter dated the 24th
inst. came to my hands yesterday noon, and
after consulting the Aldermen upon the con-
tents of it I find Capt. Lobb has been misin-
formed in regard to the contractors boat with
provisions for his Majesty's ships being stopt.
I shall therefore take the liberty to relate to
your Excellency the facts as they really happened.

Upon the gentlemen of the town and country
round having information that Capt. Lobb had
seized several vessels coming into this river
for want of stamped papers, notwithstanding
their producing certain certificates from the
several officers of the customs that no stamped
papers were to be had at the port from whence
they came, an agreement was entered into not
to supply his Majesty's ships with any more
provisions unless the particular restrictions on
this port were taken off, and in consequence of
that agreement no person would supply the
Contractor with any, so that your Excellency
will find no provisions were on board the boat.
As to the boatmen being put in gaol, it was
done by the people who had collected themselves together to procure a redress of their
grievances, and to prevent their going down,
and not only they but every other person going
to Brunswick was stopped.

Since the accommodation of matters with

9

the Commanding Officers of the King's ships,
your Excellency has no doubt been informed
that a supply of provisions has been sent them,
and your Excellency may be assured of the
best endeavors of this Corporation to forward
his Majesty's service. At the same time they
can't help expressing their concern that your
Excellency should on every occasion, lay the
whole blame of every transaction to the opposition made to the Stamp Act on this Borough,
when it is so well known the whole county has
been equally concerned in it.

I am further instructed by the corporation
to assure your Excellency that his Majesty
has not a sett of more loyal subjects in any
part of his dominions than the inhabitants of
this borough.

I am with the greatest respect Sir,
      Your Excellency's most obedient
      And most humble servant,
                MOSES JNO. DE ROSSET.

The situation, after all the excitement had
passed, is given by Governor Tryon in the two
following letters, the first addressed on the 3d
day of March to Conway, and the second, dated
April 5th, to the Lords of the Treasury:

NORTH CAROLINA,
Brunswick the 3d March 1766.

*The Right Honorable Henry Seymour Con-
way, Esq.:*

The dispatches I had the honor to direct to
you on the 25th of last month, I laid before
his Majesty's Council, as will be seen by the
extract from the Council Journal. My proclamation of the 26th past I understand has given
general satisfaction to the inhabitants concerned in the late disturbances from its mode-
ration. As I had no power to repress their
tumults it was thought most expedient not to
inflame grievances. The General Assembly I
shall prorogue from time to time till I have
the honor to receive his Majesty's further
instructions.

I find by the public papers that those Colonies who have held Assemblies in the present
times have entered warmly into disputes relative to the Stamp Act without doing any
business for his Majesty's interests, or the
benefit of the Colonies. As I have therefore
as yet had no disputes with the General Assembly, I esteem it advisable to prevent, as
much as possible, any breach in the Legislature, as by this caution I think I shall be best
able to support the honor and dignity of government till I can be informed of the resolutions taken by his Majesty and his Parliament
to terminate the present disturbances in these
provinces. If it should ever be found necessary to send military force into this Colony,

the first week in October is the soonest they
should arrive, if brought from a more northward country.   Were they to land in the heat
of summer this climate would be as fatal to
them as the climate of Pensacola has proved
to the troops sent there.   Capt Lobb has
acquainted me he has received the 25th past
twenty two days provision from the Contractor.
I have enclosed a copy of the Mayor of Wilmington's letter in answer to mine put up with
the dispatches of the 25th of February, directed
to the Mayor.

Capt Dalrymple has made his report to me
that the cannon at Fort Johnston are almost
all cleared of the spikes, and that without any
prejudice to the guns.   Mr. Randolph, Surveyor General of his Majesty's Customs, who
is now with me on his return from Charles
Town has, at my request, reinstated Mr. Pennington in his office of Comptroller for this
port. I must beg leave to mention Capt Phipps
to you, Sir, who takes charge of these dispatches and to refer you to him for any further
particulars relative to the disturbances here,
he having been present and intimately acquainted with every step that was taken. The
spirit and zeal he has shown while on this
station for his Majesty's service, and the honor
of his profession does him great credit.

I have the honor to be with great respect
and esteem, &c &c.

BRUNSWICK 5th April 1766.

The Right Hon'ble The Lords Commissioners of his Majesty's Treasury:

I was honored with your Lordships commands on the 25th of March last by the favor of Mr. Lowndes's letter of the 14th of September 1765 requiring me to give my assistance to the Distributor of the Stamps in the execution of his office. Some stamps for this province arrived here from Virginia the 28th of November last in the Diligence Sloop of War; but as Mr. Houston, Distributor of the Stamps, was obliged publicly to resign his office in the Court House of Wilmington on the 16th of the same month, a copy of which I enclose, I desired Capt Phipps to keep the stamps on board the *Diligence*. They were lately removed into his Majesty's Sloop, the *Viper*, Capt Lobb Commanding, the *Diligence* having sailed for England. My endeavors, my Lords, to promote the circulation of the stamps in this province have been accompanied with my warmest zeal, as I flatter myself the letter I wrote on that subject to Mr. Conway, one of his Majesty's principal Secretaries of State will testify. The ill success that has attended this discharge of my duty has given me real concern. Since the riotous assembly of men in Wilmington and Brunswick on the 19th, 20th and 21st of February last, there has been no disturbances in the province, the ports have never been shut, and entries and clearances are made in the form that was practiced before the Stamp Act was appointed by Parliament to take effect. I continue in opinion that these Southern provinces will regulate their further obedience and conduct agreeable to the measures that are adopted by the more formidable colonies to the Northward.

I am, my Lords, with all possible esteem and respect, &c.

The foregoing facts were well known, though only by tradition, before the discovery of Tryon's letter-book in London in 1848.

The events they describe were not, in the ordinary sense, great historical events, it is true, but they were highly creditable to the actors in them, and show conclusively that the spirit of Liberty manifested itself, to say the least, as boldly, intelligently and promptly among North Carolinians in the early days as elsewhere, and that they had as just an appreciation of their rights under the British constitution as the most enlightened subjects of the Crown at home or in the other Colonies. And yet the historians of the United States, while carefully noting similar events in the other Colonies, have, without an exception, omitted from their pages any mention of this first and only open, defiant, armed resistance to the Stamp Act which occurred in America—

just as for a long time they ignored the first
Declaration of Independence, which was proclaimed in Mecklenburg County in the same
State, and the first resolutions of a Provincial
Congress directing the Delegates to the Continental Congress to declare in favor of independence, which were passed at Halifax on
the 12th day of April, 1776, more than a month
before the celebrated resolutions of the Virginia Assembly on the same subject.

The blame for these oversights—for it is not
to be presumed that the neglect was inten-
tional—rests primarily upon the people of
North Carolina, who have ever been indifferent,
if not averse, to claiming their own from the
Muse of History.

NOTE.—As several of our historians have mentioned a certain duel fought by Captain Alex. Simpson and Lieutenant
Thomas Whitehurst of the ship *Viper*, about the time of the
Stamp-Act excitement on the Cape Fear; and as not one of
the statements given by these writers is correct, it may be well
to give a true version of the affair, as taken from the records.

Wheeler, in his history, says that in February, 1766, a duel
occurred between these parties—that Simpson sympathized
with the Colonists, and Whitechurst (Whitehurst) favored
Tryon ; that Whitehurst being killed, Simpson was arrested,
tried before Ch. J. Berry and acquitted ; that Tryon insinuated
connivance on the part of Judge Berry, summoned him before
the Council, and the Judge, in a frenzy of apprehension, com-

mitted suicide. And Wheeler quotes Martin as authority for his statement.

"Shocco" Jones, in his "Defence of North Carolina," says Simpson was condemned, but escaped and fled to England.

Moore, in his History, says that Simpson (not Whitehurst) was killed, and that Whitehurst was convicted of murder, but that Judge Berry "granted him enough time before execution to enable him to escape," and that "Tryon was furious and so wrought upon the fears of Judge Berry that he committed suicide."

In the first place, the duel occurred at Brunswick, March 18th, 1765, and was caused, not by the Stamp-Act excitement, but by a *woman*, according to Tryon's report to the Board of Trade. It was a brutal affair, in which Simpson not only broke Whitehurst's thigh with his shot, but broke his head with the butt of his pistol, breaking the butt and pan of the pistol at the same time. Simpson himself was shot behind the right shoulder, the ball coming out under his arm. The witnesses before the coroner's jury were midshipmen James Brewster and James Mooringe. Simpson escaped the night before Governor Dobbs died, 28th March, and Tryon issued a proclamation offering £50 reward for his arrest ; and wrote to Governor Fauquier of Virginia, saying that, as Simpson had some months previously married "Miss Annie Pierson, daughter of Mrs. Ramsburg, whose husband keeps a tavern in Norfolk," and as Mrs. Simpson had returned to Virginia, he suspected Simpson had gone there—that "the weak state of his health and the dangerous condition of his wound," strengthened this conjecture, and it was "not probable that he should undertake a long voyage ;" and he characterized Simpson's conduct as "extraordinary." It certainly was extraordinary, and why the seconds or witnesses permitted it is incomprehensible. Simpson afterwards surrendered himself, was tried at October Term, 1765 (a month before the stamp ship arrived), was convicted of manslaughter, and branded with the letter M on the ball of the thumb of his left hand, in open Court, and discharged—as appears by the record of the trial, still preserved at the court-house in Wilmington. The allegation that Judge Berry's sui-

cide was the result of his fright at the escape of Simpson, therefore, is wholly untrue.

In a letter to the Board of Trade, dated February 1st, 1766,
Tryon says, "Mr. Berry, Chief Justice of this Province, shot
himself in the head the 21st Decr last, and died in Wilmington
the 29th of the same month. The coroner's inquest sat on the
body and brought in a verdict 'Lunacy.'" This was two
months after Simpson's conviction, and nearly a year after the
duel. The place of Judge Berry's suicide was in a house opposite the present court-house at Wilmington.

CHAPTER IV.

1768–1771.

The Regulators' War—Its Origin and History—General Waddell's Connection with it.

THE Stamp Act was repealed in March,
1766, and on the 25th of June Governor
Tryon issued a proclamation announcing the
fact, in which—having learned some valuable
lessons in the months preceding, and having
determined to change his tactics and play a
conciliatory role—he severely denounced the
extortions which had been practiced in the
Western Counties by the officers of the Courts
and others, and sternly forbade these officers
to take more than their legal fees thereafter.
He also indulged in a somewhat tender appeal
to the people to render a cheerful obedience to
the legislative authority of the mother country.

Immediately upon the appearance of this
proclamation an amusing, and somewhat dis-
gusting, exchange of felicitations took place
between the Mayor, Recorder and Aldermen
of Wilmington, and the Governor; but each

party to this performance was conscious of the hollow insincerity of the proceedings, and each mistrusted the other. The Legislature, which had not met since May, 1765, was called together in November, and, although they expressed their pleasure at and returned thanks for the repeal of the Stamp Act, and declared their loyalty to the Crown, they did not humiliate themselves in any way. They did, however, foolishly appropriate a large amount to build a mansion for the Governor at Newbern ; but their excuse was that the Assembly had previously promised to do it, in consideration of the repeal of an act to build at Tower Hill on the Neuse. The cost of this "palace," as it was called, and as it really was, was over $75,000—an enormous sum for those times. Over the main entrance to it was a pompous Latin inscription, said to have been written by Sir Wm. Draper. General Miranda, who visited it with Judge Martin in 1783, said that his own country (South America) contained no building equal to it.

While this palace was in course of construction, and as if to aggravate the general complaint of extravagance in public expenditure, Tryon organized an escort to accompany him in personally running the boundary line between the Cherokee nation and the Province. The escort consisted of about a hundred men, selected from the Rowan and Mecklenburg regiments, the detachment from the former commanded by Lieutenant Colonel Frohock, and from the latter by Lieutenant Colonel Moses Alexander, and the whole under Colonel Hugh Waddell. There were also an Adjutant General, an Aide, and a Chaplain, all with high rank and pay. The expedition lasted nearly a month, beginning on the 19th May, 1767, and it was because of his conduct on this expedition that Tryon received from the Cherokees the *soubriquet* of " Wolf of Carolina."

Meanwhile the people, of the Western part of the Colony especially, were growing more restless under the continued exactions and extortions practiced upon them by local officers; and, notwithstanding the repeal of the Stamp Act, were, in the Eastern section, greatly dissatisfied with the Navigation Act and other embarrassments to their trade.

Even men of well known loyalty, like Hugh Waddell, were severely tried by the course affairs were taking. The discontent in the West was because of local grievances, that in the East because of the legislation of Parliament.*

A "Serious Address" had been published in Granville County, and in August, 1766, during a session of the Inferior Court of Orange, a number of men had entered the court-house and handed a paper to the Clerk to read aloud in regard to the local grievances of the people of that County.

With this event began the troubles which culminated in what is known as the "Regulators' War," a contest which, beginning in a temperate protest against the conduct of local officers, degenerated, under the leadership of a cunning and cowardly fellow, into an utterly indefensible outbreak against all law, which, if not suppressed, threatened the overthrow of

*November 15, 1767, John Crawford, member from Anson, resigned his seat and resignation accepted by House. Tryon forbore to issue writ for new election until he could hear from Home Government. Earl Hillsborough, June 11th, 1768, says he was right; that "there is no precedent of a member resigning his seat in Parliament, and the usages and precedents of the House of Commons being adopted by the Assembly of North Carolina, the House was mistaken in accepting the resignation of Crawford." This seems to verify the old maxim in regard to office-holders, viz.: "Few die, and none resign."

any form of government and the destruction of
social order. The name "Regulator" was
adopted at a meeting held at Sandy Creek, in
what was then Orange, and is now Randolph
County, on the 22d of March, 1767, at which
a written agreement was drawn up and an
association was formed "for regulating public
grievances." This agreement contemplated
no violence, and only bound the signers to pay
no more taxes until satisfied they were agreeable to law and were properly applied; to pay
no more than legal fees to any officer unless
forced to do so; to meet often for conference
with their representatives in regard to amend-
ing the laws; to elect better men to office, and
to petition the authorities for redress.

But their leader, Herman Husbands, though
uneducated, was a mischievous and turbulent
demagogue and a canting hypocrite, who,
under the garb of the Society of Friends
(Quakers), from which he was expelled for
immorality, concealed an ambitious and venom-
ous spirit. The Sandy Creek agreement was
but the first step in his programme. He
set himself diligently to work to inflame the
passions of the people, to exaggerate the evils
of which they justly complained, and to incite
them to violence. He passed most of his time

in going about haranguing crowds of the ignorant and untutored, and plied his vocation even
on Sundays.

He had a coadjutor in Edmund Fanning,
who was Colonel of the militia of Orange and
was a Court Officer who, by his extortions and
offensive conduct generally, was the most
obnoxious man in the Province. Fanning did
all he could to aggravate the Regulators, and
they repaid him with interest whenever they
could. Without reciting every detail of the
progress of the Regulators' outbreak, it will
suffice to say that after various interviews
between the agents of the Association and the
Governor, and after matters had well nigh
reached a peaceable adjustment, Husbands,
who dreaded nothing so much as the stopping
of his trade of demagogue and agitator, in-
vented a new series of grievances against a new
set of alleged criminals, namely, the members
of the Assembly and the Treasurers of the
Province. Governor Tryon laid these new
grievances before the Council, but they requested him to notify the Regulators that no
change would be made in the propositions
already submitted to them by the Governor,
which included a promise that the officers who
had been guilty of extortion should be prose-

cuted. Unfortunately for them the Regulators were guided absolutely by Husbands, who exercised an unbounded influence over them, and consequently matters remained in the same condition until the arrest and trial of Husbands for a riot at Hillsborough, where Governor Tryon, who had been inspecting the militia farther West, appeared at the head of eleven hundred men, while more than three times that number of Regulators were in the vicinity awaiting the result of the trial. While his own trial was pending, Husbands, according to his own written statement, agreed with Fanning, like a selfish and cowardly traitor, to abandon the cause of the Regulators provided he was released.

Fanning was indicted at the same term of the Court for extortion. Husbands was acquitted, and Fanning, who was probably tried by the same jury, was convicted in five cases, but was only fined a penny and costs in each case, because he pleaded a misconstruction of the statute regulating fees, and showed that he got the judgment of the County Court in his favor before taking the fees.

He ought, doubtless, to have been severely punished, and the reputation of the Court suffered in the esteem of all fair-minded men when such a judgment was pronounced. The record of one of the Judges, Maurice Moore, as a man friendly disposed to the Regulators, as well as tradition in his family, justifies the belief that he did not concur with the other two Judges in their sentence.

The trial took place in September, 1768, and, after the adjournment of Court, Tryon issued a proclamation pardoning all concerned in the late disturbances, except about a dozen who were named. In the judgment of many at that time, and of all reflecting persons now, Tryon ought to have left the violators of the law to the prosecuting officers and the Courts, until their acts assumed more serious proportions, which they did a year or so afterwards.

During the year 1769 the spirit of the Regulators, which the proceedings of the Court at Hillsborough appeared only to aggravate, manifested itself in new acts of violence, and although, by the express order of the British Ministry, Tryon issued on the 9th of September an additional proclamation of pardon to everybody, without exception, who had been concerned in the Regulators' disturbances, these disturbances continued, and the service of process by the sheriffs and their deputies became nearly impossible. The Regulators

10

having petitioned the Governor for a new Assembly he granted it, and the new Assembly met in October, 1769. The Regulators had elected enough members of this body to effect a change of about thirty votes. This body was soon dissolved by the Governor.

New organizations of the Regulators were formed, and they had extended over a wide area by the beginning of the year 1770. In the region around Salisbury, as reported by Judge Moore, who held Court there in March, it was impossible to collect taxes or levy an execution, which, as he said, were "plain proofs, among others, that their designs have extended further than to promote public inquiry into the conduct of public affairs." At Hillsboro, in September, when the Court met, with Judge Henderson presiding, the greatest outrage or series of outrages yet perpetrated by the Regulators took place. They insulted and cruelly beat some members of the bar, and going into the court-house in a riotous manner, with Husbands at their head, they demanded of Judge Henderson that he should try their leaders, and should take the jury from their number.

The Judge adjourned the Court and that night fled the town. They then held a mock court, and made scandalous entries on the docket. On the 12th of November they burned Judge Henderson's barn, and on the 14th his house. Again a new Assembly was called, and met at Newbern in December, 1770. It provided, from the first, for relief to the people by various acts, one of which was to refund the amount of taxes alleged to have been illegally collected since 1768.

Threats having been made by the Regulators that they would go to Newbern, where the Legislature was in session, to prevent Fanning from being seated as a member, the Governor called out the militia, and the trenches were manned for the protection of the Legislature.

Afterwards, when Husbands, who was a member from Orange, was expelled for lying and for threatening the Assembly with the Regulators in case of his confinement by the House, it was ascertained that the Regulators were actually preparing to justify these threats by marching to Newbern.

Again, when the Assembly was about to adjourn, news came that the Regulators were in large force at Cross Creek (now Fayetteville) and had declared their purpose to go to Newbern and burn the Governor's "palace." Thereupon the Assembly voted the Governor means of defence. These threats were not carried into execution, but the disorders grew worse continually, and other Judges were beaten and Courts broken up.

It now became evident that but one course remained to be pursued towards the Regulators, if government of any kind was to be maintained in North Carolina, and accordingly the Governor, *urged by the Council, the Courts, and the Legislature*,* made his preparations to march against the Regulators and put an end to their outrages.

He assembled about eleven hundred men, composed of detachments from the counties in the East, and from Wake, and marched to Orange. The Regulators numbered about two thousand. They met near the banks of the Alamance. Notwithstanding the conduct of the Regulators in cruelly flogging two of the Governor's officers (Captains Walker and Ashe), whom they had captured while on a scouting expedition, the course of the Governor, according to every account of the affair, exhibited the utmost aversion to shedding blood. Messengers had passed between the forces, seeking a reconciliation in vain. On

*See note at the end of this chapter.

the 16th of May they had approached within a half mile of each other, and the Governor sent a message demanding unconditional surrender. Husbands, who was still the leader of the Regulators, returned his defiance and seemed determined to fight.

They came within one hundred yards of each other, and the Governor made a civil and a military officer read a proclamation in the nature of a riot act. They then approached until the ranks passed each other, making a retrograde movement necessary to regain their places. They then stood for an hour, at a distance of twenty-five yards, quarreling and abusing each other, when the comedy was ended by the furious shout of the Governor: "Fire! fire on them or on me," and the battle began. Husbands, like the cowardly cur he was, immediately fled; those of his followers who did not follow his example took to the trees, Indian fashion, and in a little while afterwards were routed.

Before and during the fight the Governor had sent flags of truce, both of which were shot down. His loss was nine killed and sixty wounded; that of the Regulators was twenty killed and an unknown number wounded.

Previous to Tryon's expedition to the Alamance in 1771,* Waddell had been promoted
to the rank of General, and was the ranking
officer of the Province, and the most experienced officer in it, although not yet thirty-
five years old.   Preparatory to that expedition
he had been sent to Salisbury to take command
of a force which was to co-operate with the
troops under Tryon's immediate command,

---

*[TRYON'S LETTER-BOOK.]

NO. 70. EARL HILLSBOROUGH.

NEWBERN 12 April 1771

*   *   *   *   *   *   *   *   *   *   *

The next day, the 18th [March] I summoned His Majesty's
Council, related to them some reasons that prompted me to
offer my service, and took their advice on the expediency of
raising forces to restore peace and stability to government.
They approving the measure I lost no time in sending requisi-
tions to almost every County in the province for certain quotas
of men, &c., &c., &c.

*   *   *   *   *   *   *   *   *   *

To forward this business I went myself last week to Wilmington when I appointed Mr. Waddell General of all the
forces raised, or to be raised against the insurgents, and expect
he will get seven hundred men from the Western Counties to
serve under his immediate command, who will march them
into the settlement of the insurgents by the way of Salisbury
while I bring up the forces from the Southern and Eastern
parts, and break into their settlements on the east side of
Orange County.   In my excursion to Wilmington I had the
satisfaction to find the gentlemen and inhabitants of Cape Fear
unanimous and spirited in the cause, and the officers successful
in recruiting.   *   *   *   *   *   *

who went from the low country and from Wake
County. He was waiting for the arrival of
some ammunition wagons, which had to make
the long journey from Charleston, S. C., before
starting with his force.

When the wagons, four in number, reached
Phifer's Hill, near Concord, they were seized
and the ammunition was destroyed by some
daring young fellows calling themselves
"Black Boys," under the leadership of James
White, who was afterwards a brave officer in
the Revolution.

These young men sympathized with the
Regulators who, as they had been led to believe,
were merely resisting oppression, and were
guilty of no lawlessness or other crime. The
loss of his ammunition was the first serious
difficulty that General Waddell encountered,
but when he started with three hundred and
forty men to join Tryon, and had reached a
point a few miles beyond the Yadkin river, he
discovered a large force, a much larger one
than his own, which had been gathered to
oppose his march, and which was ready for a
fight. The officers in General Waddell's command were, Griffith Rutherford (afterwards a
distinguished Revolutionary officer, who attained the rank of Brigadier General), William

Lindsay, Adlai Alexander, Thomas Neal, Frederick Ross, Robert Shaw, Samuel Spencer, Robert Harris, Samuel Snead, and William Luckie. These officers held a council of war, and drew up a paper which they signed, dated "General Waddell's Camp, Potts' Creek, 10th May, 1771," which reads as follows:

By a Council of officers of the Western detachment, considering the great superiority of the insurgents in number, and the resolution of a great part of their own men not to fight, it was resolved that they should retreat across the Yadkin.

It was also discovered that many of the detachment were communicating with the Regulators, and thereupon General Waddell retreated. He then sent a dispatch to Tryon acquainting him with the situation of affairs, and Tryon, who was a fearless and skillful officer, immediately moved on the Regulators, and the "battle" of Alamance, on the 16th May, ended the so-called Regulators' war.

General Waddell was not present at the Alamance affair, and was doubtless glad of it, for, while his duty as an officer was plain, he, like Caswell, Ashe, Howe, and others, whose patriotism was displayed in the Revolution so soon afterwards, was averse to shedding the blood of any American, even to sustain just authority, and, like them, he was a true friend of liberty. But the conduct of the Regulators forced the issue between law and mob rule, and left no alternative to the authorities but the prompt suppression of them by force.

Notwithstanding the overwhelming evidence spread upon the records, and the unanimous judgment of all the writers upon the subject, including the two ablest apologists of the Regulators, Caruthers and Wiley, the belief has prevailed to some extent in North Carolina, and very generally outside of the State, that the Regulators were a body of patriots whose zeal in the cause of liberty could brook no restraint, and that they poured out the first libation to her on American soil, at the battle of Alamance in May, 1771, in resistance to British oppression. This is a total perversion of the truth of history, and not only does gross injustice, but actually reverses the position of parties in the Revolution.

The truth in regard to the Regulators is contained in the following propositions, viz:

First. That they were but a small minority of the people of North Carolina.

Second. That they contended for no great principle.

Third. That, with two or three exceptions, there was not a man prominent for intellect or virtue in their organization.

Fourth. That they were not republicans.

Fifth. That they were Tories in the Revolution; and

Sixth. That they were opposed by the prominent Whig leaders of that day, including such men as Griffith Rutherford, Willie Jones and others, who, after the Revolution, were suspected of radicalism.

1. Proof of the first proposition will not be required by any one at all acquainted with the subject.

2. The grievances complained of by the Regulators were purely local, and arose out of the extortions and malpractice of the sheriffs, clerks, registers of deeds and tax-collectors. The offenders were their fellow-subjects and neighbors, and not the King and Parliament, to whom they declared their loyalty and devotion in the strongest terms, and proved it by being Tories in the Revolution. The taxes against which they protested were not *British* taxes, illegally imposed, but taxes imposed by their own representatives in the Assembly— representatives with whom, as declared in the Sandy Creek Association, they proposed to

confer, and whom they proposed to displace with better men if they did not do right. And if the original purposes of that Association had been carried out in good faith—if by concerted action they had persistently indicted offenders against the law, and had sued for the penalties provided by the statute (Westminster I), and had tested the legality of seizures and the like, instead of resorting to a "higher law" of their own, and enlisting and training men, and breaking up the Courts, and whipping Judges and attorneys, and attempting with armed force to overawe the Legislature, and committing other similar outrages—they would have escaped the fate that befel them, and would have appeared in history in a very different light.

3. The third proposition—that with two or three exceptions, their organization embraced no man prominent for intellect or virtue—cannot be denied.

The discussion of historical questions ought to be approached without prejudice or improper motives of any kind; and, therefore, while it is natural and commendable in the descendants of the Regulators to seek to vindicate their conduct, the effort cannot be justified either by distorting facts, or by imputing false or unworthy motives to others. It has been said that some of the "gentry," as some of the Eastern men were invidiously called, had aided in suppressing the Regulators because of offended pride at not having been consulted upon or placed in charge of the movement. There is no foundation whatever for this strange assertion, and it must be attributed, like many of the so-called facts which filial piety has supplied in regard to the Regulators, to a loose tradition, based upon unjust prejudices. The persons to whom allusion is made as the "gentry," were, almost without exception, men who owed nothing to the accidents of birth or fortune, but had earned positions of respectability by their public services, their superior intelligence and force of character.

Those who are unable or unwilling to reconcile the conduct of these "gentry"—who in 1765 denounced and resisted with arms the Stamp Act and other legislation of Parliament hostile to America—with their subsequent suppression of the Regulators in 1771, confuse events which are unconnected with each other, which arose from different causes and were based on different principles.

The men of 1765, as British subjects, and

in the assertion of their rights as such, resisted
the tyranny and oppression of the Crown and
Parliament, and proved their determination to
preserve their liberties. In 1768–'71, although
sympathizing with the Regulators in their
local troubles, and having contempt for the
officers who practiced extortion and other vil-
lainies upon them, they held in equal contempt
such pestilent demagogues as Husbands, who,
under the guise of virtuous indignation against
these local grievances, was instigating the
more ignorant people to resist lawful authority—thereby confounding right with wrong,
and legitimate with illegimate power, and
bringing about a state of anarchy in the Province. And when, under his leadership, those
misguided people undertook to stop the wheels
of government—when they broke up the
Courts, mobbed the Judges, whipped the
attorneys, defied the sheriffs to serve any kind
of process, and finally took up arms and organized themselves into a lawless mob, defiant of
all authority except their own will—*then*, upon
the call of the Governor, in pursuance of an
Act of Assembly, and in the performance of a
plain duty as officers and citizens who were
bound to maintain the peace and good order of
society, they went to meet force with force, and

to suppress a revolt, which—although based upon just provocation against individuals in its incipiency—had assumed proportions and was contemplating purposes inconsistent with the preservation of the forms of government, or in other words, which meant naked anarchy.

The warmest apologist of the Regulators has never justified the lawless and cruel acts perpetrated by them—their gathering in arms to overawe the Legislature and rescue Husbands, who had been expelled from that body and afterwards imprisoned, and the various other acts leading up to the battle of Alamance.

The author of the latest history of North Carolina*—who, it is proper to say, is in no way related to the men of the same name from the Cape Fear country who figured in the troubles of those times, and is not amenable to the charge of inherited prejudice—speaking of these events, says:

These misguided people, however much justified in their original movements, had become an intolerable nuisance—an impediment alike to legislation and the administration of public justice. * * * Brutal mobs ranged unchallenged from where Raleigh now stands to Charlotte.

*Major John W. Moore.

And again he says:

It has been the habit in North Carolina to assail the motives of Governor Tryon for the military movements which he inaugurated in the month of March. Whatever may have been his previous errors and mistakes, there can be no rational denial of his eminent prudence and propriety on this occasion. The Judges of the Courts, His Majesty's Council, and the House of Assembly all joined in insisting that he should raise the forces of the Province and abate a nuisance that was making North Carolina a stench in the nostrils of all civilized communities. Though the Regulation was first planned in resistance to the meanest of tyrannies, it had become the enemy of all true liberty and order, and was only the tool of one base and designing man.

The conduct, therefore, of the "gentry" in resisting the usurpations of the King and Parliament on the one hand, and in aiding to put down lawlessness on the other, commend them to the profound respect of the historian as men who had a just appreciation of true liberty; and the stigma of being gentlemen, which is sought to be affixed to their names, and memory will serve the double purpose of presenting them in their true character, and of verifying the assertion that the best men of the Province were all on one side, and that

was the side of law and legitimate rule. As
to the leaders of the Regulators—in connection
with the proposition that there were, with two
or three exceptions, no prominent men among
them—it is to be observed that the mere fact
that Husbands was the ruling spirit among
them is of itself almost conclusive evidence of
the truth of the assertion. As to his character
there is no difference of opinion, and as evidence of it very different authorities are now
given.

Governor Tryon wrote to the Earl of Hillsborough in 1768: "Not a person of the character of a gentleman appeared among these
insurgents. Herman Husbands appears to
have planned their operations; he is of a fac-
tious temper and has long since been expelled
from the Society of the Quakers for the immorality of his life."

Dr. Caruthers, the ablest apologist of the
Regulators, admits that Husbands was not at
that time in membership with the Quakers,
although he had been; and Dr. Wiley, another
apologist, says Husbands "was not a character worthy of much commendation." He
was afterwards an active insurgent in the
Whiskey Insurrection in Pennsylvania, which
was suppressed by Washington. The two or

three exceptions which qualify the third
proposition above advanced, were made out of
regard to some statements to be found in the
pages of several writers on the subject of the
Regulators' War, but an examination of the
sources of information on which they rely,
does not seem to warrant those statements in
the unqualified form in which they appear.
Not one of these excepted parties ever appeared
in arms with the Regulators, or ever took part
in their public acts, however much they may
have indulged in expressions of sympathy
with them in their troubles. There is no evidence that they approved of the lawlessness
and cruelty perpetrated by them. An idea
once prevailed, and, perhaps, still prevails,
that as the Rev. Dr. Caldwell was a mediator
between the Regulators and the Governor, the
members of the Presbyterian Church endorsed
the Regulators and joined their ranks, and
Messrs. Caruthers and Wiley, both of whom
were Presbyterian ministers, have, in defending the movement, strengthened the impression
alluded to. But the facts do not warrant the
conclusion. There were some members of Dr.
Caldwell's charge among the Regulators, and
Dr. Caldwell, an influential minister, was supposed to be in sympathy with them; but his

11

sympathy was not with them as Regulators, for even Caruthers, his biographer, says that he disapproved of and condemned their measures.

As a christian minister, he pitied them in distress and danger and tried to mitigate their punishment, but it is unjust to his memory to connect him any farther than this with the insurrection; and it is equally unjust to the Presbyterians of that day to fix upon them any part of the responsibility. Four ministers of that church in 1768 wrote letters which Col. Osborn read to the troops when defending the Government, and Tryon himself wrote to Lord Hillsborough in December, 1768: "His Majesty's Presbyterian subjects showed themselves very loyal on this service, and I have a pleasure in acknowledging the utility that the Presbyterian ministers' letters to their brethren had upon the then face of public affairs."

4. That the Regulators were not republicans is evident, both from their acts and declarations. They declared in an address to the Governor and Council, as follows: "We assure you that neither disloyalty to the best of Kings, nor dissatisfaction to the wholesomest constitution, nor yet dissatisfaction to the Legislature, gave rise to those commotions which now make so much noise."

They declared their opposition to the Judges because they had not been appointed by the King, and, according to the affidavit of Robert Lytle, they drank "damnation to King George *and success to the Pretender*," in 1770. In addition to this they "eagerly" took the oath of allegiance after their defeat at Alamance, and subsequently became active Tories (with very rare exceptions) in the Revolution.

5. When the Revolutionary War broke out in North Carolina the new Governor, Martin, relied for support almost entirely on the Highlanders and Regulators, and he was not disappointed, for he found them zealous loyalists and cordial haters of the Whigs. The latter, when the Provincial Congress was called together by Samuel Johnston on the 20th of August, 1775, at Hillsborough, apprehended an attack from the Regulators. The fear was general among the members of that body that an attempt would be made to disperse them. If the Regulators were republicans and friends of the cause, how can this apprehension on the part of the Congress be accounted for? One Colson, who was, perhaps, the leader (and certainly was a prominent member) of the Regulators after Husbands fled, surrendered himself to that Congress, and, according to a

letter written by Governor Johnston, "with every appearance of humility and contrition, even to the shedding of tears, has promised for the future to exert himself with as much assiduity in favor of our measures, *as he has hitherto in opposition to them.*"

Thus the *status* of the Regulators is fixed, and, according to the evidence furnished by these two incidents—the apprehension of an attack on the Congress and the surrender of Colson—they were necessarily either Tories or banditti. The history of individuals will not be traced.

6th. The sixth and last proposition was, that they were opposed by the prominent Whig leaders of that day; even by such men as Griffith Rutherford and Willie Jones, who were considered ultra republicans after the Revolution.

No better test of popularity could be appealed to than was furnished by the men who, having opposed and suppressed the Regulators, became afterwards favorite officers in the Revolution; and it is only necessary to mention some of their names, with the rank they attained, to prove it. (General Waddell died before the Revolution broke out, and, therefore, is not included.) John Ashe and Robert

Howe became Major Generals; Francis Nash,
Richard Caswell, James Moore, Alexander
Lillington and Griffith Rutherford became
Brigadier Generals; others became Colonels,
Abner Nash became Major, and, like Caswell,
afterwards Governor of the State.

Justice, therefore, to the memory of these
men who were before, during, and after the
Regulators' War, prominent as the enemies of
oppression and true patriots, requires that that
outbreak which they suppressed should appear
upon the page of history in its true light,
viz.: as a lawless and seditious attempt to
throw off the restraints of civilization and
to redress grievances—which certainly existed—by mob law.

With the suppression of the Regulators the
military career of General Waddell—which
had extended over sixteen years, and had taken
him from Fort Du Quesne on the Western
border of Pennsylvania, to the Savannah river
on the Southern border of South Carolina, and
into Tennessee—ended.

It is no part of the purpose of the writer to
attempt a vindication of Governor Tryon, except so far as his performance of a plain duty in
suppressing an outbreak which threatened ruin
to the Province was concerned. His conduct,

after suppressing it, was cruel and heartless, as well as contemptible and ridiculous. The execution of six prisoners at Hillsborough, including a wretched lunatic who was, tradition says, made a maniac by personal wrongs of the most infamous character perpetrated by some official, was as cruel as it was unnecessary.

Tryon left North Carolina about a month after the battle of Alamance, to become Governor of New York, and about the same time a letter, signed "Atticus," appeared in the newspapers and was widely circulated throughout the country. This letter was written by Judge Maurice Moore, and added greatly to his reputation as a lawyer and writer of brilliant talents. As it not only depicted Tryon's character in vivid colors, but gave the best history of his administration, and was written by one who, although appointed a Judge by him and required, in the discharge of his official duties, to try such cases as were brought before him, had a very just estimate of the Governor; and as it has not been published in fifty years, it is here given in full:

To his Excellency William Tryon, Esquire:

I am too well acquainted with your character to suppose you can bear to be told of your faults with temper. You are too much of the soldier, and too little of the philosopher, for reprehension. With this opinion of your Excellency, I have more reason to believe that this letter will be more serviceable to the province of New York, than useful or entertaining to its governor. The beginning of your administration in this province was marked with oppression and distress to its inhabitants. These, Sir, I do not place to your account; they are derived from higher authority than yours. You were, however, a dull, yet willing instrument, in the hands of the British Ministry to promote the means of both. You called together some of the principal inhabitants of your neighborhood, and in a strange, inverted, self-affecting speech, told them that you had left your native country, friends, and connexions, and taken upon yourself the government of North Carolina with no other view than to serve it. In the next breath, Sir, you advised them to submit to the Stamp Act, and become slaves. How could you reconcile such baneful advice with such friendly professions? But, Sir, self-contradictions with you have not been confined to words only; they have been equally extended to actions. On other occasions you have played the governor with an air of greater dignity and importance than any of your predecessors; on this, your Excellency was meanly content to solicit the currency of stamped paper in private companies. But, alas! ministerial approbation is the first wish

of your heart; it is the best security you have
for your office. Engaged as you were in this
disgraceful negotiation, the more important
duties of the governor were forgotten, or wil-
fully neglected. In murmuring, discontent,
and public confusion, you left the colony committed to your care, for near eighteen months
together, without calling an assembly. The
Stamp Act repealed, you called one; and a
fatal one it was! Under every influence your
character afforded you, at this Assembly, was
laid the foundation of all the mischief which
has since befallen this unhappy province. A
grant was made to the crown of five thousand
pounds, to erect a house for the residence of a
governor; and you, Sir, were solely intrusted
with the management of it. The infant and
impoverished state of this country could not
afford to make such a grant, and it was your
duty to have been acquainted with the circumstances of the colony you governed. This
trust proved equally fatal to the interest of the
province and to your Excellency's honor. You
made use of it, Sir, to gratify your vanity, at
the expense of both. It at once afforded you
an opportunity of leaving an elegant monu-
ment of your taste in building behind you,
and giving the ministry an instance of your
great influence and address in your new government. You, therefore, regardless of every
moral, as well as legal obligation, changed the
plan of a province-house to that of a palace,
worthy the residence of a prince of the blood,

and augmented the expense to fifteen thousand
pounds. Here, Sir, you betrayed your trust,
disgracefully to the governor, and dishonora-
bly to the man. This liberal and ingenious
stroke in politics may, for all I know, have
promoted you to the government of New York.
Promotion may have been the reward of such
sort of merit. Be this as it may, you reduced
the next Assembly you met to the unjust
alternative of granting ten thousand pounds
more, or sinking the five thousand they had
already granted. They chose the former. It
was most pleasing to the governor, but directly
contrary to the sense of their constituents.
This public imposition upon a people, who,
from poverty, were hardly able to pay the
necessary expenses of government, occasioned
general discontent, which your Excellency,
with wonderful address, improved into a civil
war.

In a colony without money, and among a
people, almost desperate with distress, public
profusion should have been carefully avoided;
but unfortunately for the country, you were
bred a soldier, and have a natural, as well as
acquired fondness for military parade. You
were intrusted to run a Cherokee boundary
about ninety miles in length; this little service at once afforded you an opportunity of
exercising your military talents, and making
a splendid exhibition of yourself to the Indians.
To a gentleman of your Excellency's turn of
mind, this was no unpleasing prospect; you

marched to perform it, in a time of profound
peace, at the head of a company of militia, in
all the pomp of war, and returned with the
honorable title, conferred on you by the Cherokees, of *Great Wolf of North Carolina*. This
line of marked trees, and your Excellency's
prophetic title, cost the province a greater sum
than two pence a head, on all the taxable persons in it for one year, would pay.

Your next expedition, Sir, was a more
important one.   Four or five hundred ignorant
people, who called themselves Regulators, took
it into their head to quarrel with their representative, a gentleman honored with your
Excellency's esteem.   They foolishly charged
him with every distress they felt; and, in
revenge, shot two or three musket balls through
his house.   They at the same time rescued a
horse which had been seized for the public tax.
These crimes were punishable in the courts of
law, and at that time the criminals were amenable to legal process.   Your Excellency and
your confidential friends, it seems, were of a
different opinion.   All your duty could possibly require of you on this occasion, if it required
any thing at all, was to direct a prosecution
against th offenders.   You should have carefully avoided becoming a party in the dispute.
But, Sir, your genius could not lie still; you
enlisted yourself a volunteer in this service,
and entered into a negotiation with the Regulators, which at once disgraced you and encouraged them.   They despised the governor who

had degraded his own character by taking part
in a private quarrel, and insulted the man
whom they considered as personally their
enemy. The terms of accommodation your
Excellency had offered them were treated with
contempt. What they were, I never knew;
they could not have related to public offences;
these belong to another jurisdiction. All hopes
of settling the mighty contest by treaty ceasing, you prepared to decide it by means more
agreeable to your martial disposition, an appeal
to the sword. You took the field in September,
1768, at the head of ten or twelve hundred men,
and published an oral manifesto, the substance
of which was, that you had taken up arms to
protect a superior court of justice from insult.
Permit me here to ask you, Sir, why you were
apprehensive for the court? Was the court
apprehensive for itself? Did the judges, or the
attorney-general, address your Excellency for
protection? So far from it, Sir, if these gentlemen are to be believed, they never entertained
the least suspicion of any insult, unless it was
that which they afterwards experienced from
the undue influence you offered to extend to
them, and the military display of drums, colors,
and guards, with which they were surrounded
and disturbed. How fully has your conduct,
on a like occasion since, testified that you
acted in this instance from passion, and not
from principle! In September, 1770, the Regulators forcibly obstructed the proceedings of
Hillsborough Superior Court, obliged the offi-

cers to leave it, and blotted out the records. A
little before the next term, when their contempt
of courts was sufficiently proved, you wrote an
insolent letter to the judges, and attorney-
general, commanding them to attend to it.
Why did you not protect the court at this time?
You will blush at the answer, Sir. The conduct of the Regulators, at the preceding term,
made it more than probable that those gentlemen would be insulted at this, and you were
not unwilling to sacrifice them to increase the
guilt of your enemies.

Your Excellency said that you had armed
to protect a court. Had you said to revenge
the insult you and your friends had received,
it would have been more generally credited in
this country. The men, for the trial of whom
the court was thus extravagantly protected, of
their own accord, squeezed through a crowd of
soldiers, and surrendered themselves, as if they
were bound to do so by their recognizance.

Some of these people were convicted, fined,
and imprisoned, which put an end to a piece
of knight-errantry, equally aggravating to the
populace and burthensome to the country. On
this occasion, Sir, you were alike successful in
the diffusion of a military spirit through the
colony and in the warlike exhibition you set
before the public; you at once disposed the
vulgar to hostilities, and proved the legality of
arming, in cases of dispute, by example. Thus
warranted by precedent and tempered by sympathy, popular discontent soon became resent-

ment and opposition; revenge superseded justice, and force the laws of the country; courts
of law were treated with contempt, and government itself set at defiance. For upwards
of two months was the frontier part of the
country left in a state of perfect anarchy.
Your Excellency then thought fit to consult
the representatives of the people, who presented you a bill which you passed into a law.
The design of this act was to punish past riots
in a new jurisdiction, to create new offences
and to secure the collection of the public tax;
which, ever since the province had been sad-
dled with a palace, the Regulators had refused
to pay. The jurisdiction for holding pleas of
all capital offences was, by a former law, confined to the particular district in which they
were committed. This act did not change that
jurisdiction; yet your Excellency, in the ful-
ness of your power, established a new one for
the trial of such crimes in a different district.
Whether you did this through ignorance or
design can only be determined in your own
breast; it was equally violative of a sacred
right, every British subject is entitled to, of
being tried by his neighbours, and a positive
law of the province you yourself had ratified.
In this foreign jurisdiction, bills of indictment
were preferred, and found, as well for felonies
as riots against a number of Regulators; they
refused to surrender themselves within the
time limited by the riot act, and your Excellency opened your third campaign. These

indictments charged the crimes to have been
committed in Orange County, in a distinct
district from that in which the court was held.
The superior court law prohibits prosecution
for capital offences in any other district than
that in which they were committed. What
distinctions the gentlemen of the long robe
might make on such an occasion I do not
know, but it appears to me those indictments
might as well have been found in your Excellency's kitchen; and give me leave to tell you,
Sir, that a man is not bound to answer to a
charge that a court has no authority to make,
nor doth the law punish a neglect to perform
that which it does not command. The riot
act declared those only outlawed who refused
to answer to indictments legally found. Those
who had been capitally charged were illegally
indicted, and could not be outlaws; yet your
Excellency proceeded against them as such.
I mean to expose your blunders, not to defend
their conduct; that was as insolent and daring
as the desperate state your administration had
reduced them to could possibly occasion. I am
willing to give you full credit for every service
you have rendered this country. Your active
and gallant behaviour, in extinguishing the
flame you yourself had kindled, does you great
honor. For once your military talents were
useful to the province; you bravely met in the
field, and vanquished, an host of scoundrels,
whom you had made intrepid by abuse. It
seems difficult to determine, Sir, whether your

Excellency is more to be admired for your skill in creating the cause, or your bravery in suppressing the effect. This single action would have blotted out for ever half the evils of your administration; but alas! Sir, the conduct of the general after his victory, was more disgraceful to the hero who obtained it, than that of the man before it had been to the governor. Why did you stain so great an action with the blood of a prisoner who was in a state of insanity? The execution of James Few was inhuman; that miserable wretch was entitled to life till nature, or the laws of his country, deprived him of it. The battle of the Allemance was over; the soldier was crowned with success, and the peace of the province restored. There was no necessity for the infamous example of an arbitrary execution, without judge or jury. I can freely forgive you, Sir, for killing Robert Thompson, at the beginning of the battle; he was your prisoner, and was making his escape to fight against you. The laws of self-preservation sanctified the action, and justly entitle your Excellency to an act of indemnity.

The sacrifice of Few, under the criminal circumstances, could neither atone for his crime nor abate your rage; this task was reserved for his unhappy parents. Your vengeance, Sir, in this instance, it seems, moved in a retrograde direction to that proposed in the second commandment against idolaters; you visited the sins of the child upon the father,

and, for want of the third and fourth generation to extend it to, collaterally divided it
between brothers and sisters. The heavy
affliction, with which the untimely death of a
son had burthened his parents, was sufficient
to have cooled the resentment of any man,
whose heart was susceptible of the feelings of
humanity; yours, I am afraid, is not a heart
of that kind. If it is, why did you add
to the distresses of that family? Why refuse
the petition of the town of Hillsborough in
favor of them, and unrelentingly destroy, as
far as you could, the means of their future
existence? It was cruel, Sir, and unworthy a
soldier.

Your conduct to others after your success,
whether it respected person or property, was
as lawless as it was unnecessarily expensive
to the colony. When your Excellency had
exemplified the power of government in the
death of a hundred Regulators, the survivors,
to a man, became proselytes to government;
they readily swallowed your new-coined oath,
to be obedient to the laws of the province, and
to pay the public taxes. It is a pity, Sir, that
in devising this oath, you had not attended to
the morals of those people. You might easily
have restrained every criminal inclination, and
have made them good men, as well as good
subjects. The battle of the Allemance had
equally disposed them to moral and to political
conversion; there was no necessity, Sir, when
the people were reduced to obedience, to ravage
the country, or to insult individuals.

Had your Excellency nothing else in view than to enforce a submission to the laws of the country, you might safely have disbanded the army within ten days after your victory; in that time the chiefs of the Regulators were run away, and their deluded followers had returned to their homes. Such a measure would have saved the province twenty thousand pounds at least. But, Sir, you had farther employment for the army; you were, by an extraordinary bustle in administering oaths, and disarming the country, to give a serious appearance of rebellion to the outrage of a mob; you were to aggravate the importance of your own services by changing a general dislike of your administration into disaffection to his Majesty's person and government, and the riotous conduct that dislike had occasioned into premeditated rebellion. This scheme, Sir, is really an ingenious one; if it succeeds, you may possibly be rewarded for your services with the honor of knighthood.

From the 16th of May to the 16th of June, you were busied in securing the allegiance of rioters, and levying contributions of beef and flour. You occasionally amused yourself with burning a few houses, treading down corn, insulting the suspected, and holding courts-martial. These courts took cognizance of civil as well as military offences, and even extended their jurisdiction to ill-breeding and want of good manners. One Johnston, who was a reputed Regulator, but whose greatest crime,

12

I believe, was writing an impudent letter to
your lady, was sentenced, in one of these military courts, to receive five hundred lashes, and
received two hundred and fifty of them accordingly. But, Sir, however exceptionable your
conduct may have been on this occasion, it
bears little proportion to that which you
adopted on the trial of the prisoners you had
taken. These miserable wretches were to be
tried for a crime made capital by a temporary
act of Assembly of twelve months' duration.
That act had, in great tenderness to his Majesty's subjects, converted riots into treasons.
A rigorous and punctual execution of it was
as unjust as it was politically unnecessary.
The terror of the examples now proposed to
be made under it was to expire, with the law,
in less than nine months after. The suffer-
ings of these people could therefore amount to
little more than mere punishment to themselves. Their offences were derived from
public and from private impositions; and they
were the followers, not the leaders, in the
crimes they had committed. Never were
criminals more justly entitled to every lenity
the law could afford them; but, Sir, no consideration could abate your zeal in a cause you
had transferred from yourself to your sover-
eign. You shamefully exerted every influence
of your character against the lives of these
people. As soon as you were told that an in-
dulgence of one day had been granted by the
court to two men to send for witnesses, who

actually established their innocence, and saved
their lives, you sent an aid-de-camp to the
judges and attorney-general, to acquaint them
that you were dissatisfied with the inactivity
of their conduct, and threatened to represent
them unfavorably in England if they did not
proceed with more spirit and despatch. Had
the court submitted to influence, all testimony
on the part of the prisoners would have been
excluded ; they must have been condemned, to
a man. You said that your solicitude for the
condemnation of these people arose from your
desire of manifesting the lenity of government
in their pardon. How have your actions con-
tradicted your words! Out of twelve that were
condemned, the lives of six only were spared.
Do you know, Sir, that your lenity on this
occasion was less than that of the bloody
Jeffries in 1685? He condemned five hundred
persons, but saved the lives of two hundred
and seventy.

In the execution of the six devoted offenders,
your Excellency was as short of General Kirk
in form, as you were of Judge Jeffries in lenity.
That general honored the execution he had
the charge of with play of pipes, sound of
trumpets, and beat of drums; you were content with the silent display of colors only.
The disgraceful part you acted in this ceremony, of pointing out the spot for erecting the
gallows, and clearing the field around for
drawing up the army in form, has left a ridiculous idea of your character behind you, which

bears a strong resemblance to that of a busy
undertaker at a funeral. This scene closed
your Excellency's administration in this country, to the great joy of every man in it, a few
of your own contemptible tools only excepted.

Were I personally your Excellency's enemy,
I would follow you into the shade of life, and
show you equally the object of pity and contempt to the wise and serious, and of jest and
ridicule to the ludicrous and sarcastic. Truly
pitiable, Sir, is the pale and trembling impa-
tience of your temper. No character, however
distinguished for wisdom and virtue, can sanc-
tify the least degree of contradiction to your
political opinions. On such occasions, Sir, in
a rage, you renounce the character of a gentleman, and precipitately mark the most exalted
merit with every disgrace the haughty inso-
lence of a governor can inflict upon it. To
this unhappy temper, Sir, may be ascribed
most of the absurdities of your administration
in this country. It deprived you of every
assistance men of spirit and abilities could have
given you, and left you, with all your passions
and inexperience about you, to blunder through
the duties of your office, supported and approved by the most profound ignorance and
abject servility.

Your pride has as often exposed you to ridicule, as the rude petulance of your disposition
has to contempt. Your solicitude about the
title of *Her Excellency* for Mrs. Tryon, and
the arrogant reception you gave to a respect-

able company at an entertainment of your own making, seated with your lady by your side on elbow-chairs, in the middle of the ball-room, bespeak a littleness of mind, which, believe me, Sir, when blended with the dignity and importance of your office, renders you truly ridiculous.

High stations have often proved fatal to those who have been promoted to them; yours, Sir, has proved so to you. Had you been contented to pass through life in a subordinate military character, with the private virtues you have, you might have lived serviceable to your country, and reputable to yourself; but, Sir, when, with every disqualifying circumstance, you took upon you the government of a province, though you gratified your ambition, you made a sacrifice of yourself.

Yours, &c.

ATTICUS.

In an old volume, containing a number of pamphlets and letters of the Revolutionary period, which has recently come into the writer's possession, there are some amusing criticisms of Tryon, written from New York by a Loyalist. In one letter, dated December 10th, 1777, the writer says that Tryon's injudicious conduct had been of infinite prejudice to the British cause—that he followed the army everywhere, administering oaths of allegiance, and "puffing off his assiduity;" and

that as one method of converting the rebels he
sent out officers with flags of truce, loaded
down with *sermons* to distribute among them—
"with which sermons the rebels light their
tobacco-pipes, or expend them in other necessary uses." Again he says: "Governor, now
General, Tryon, who is the pink of politeness,
and the quintescence of vanity, chose to dis-
tinguish himself by petitioning that the Provincials under his command should occupy the
outposts at Kingsbridge; he had his wish for a
long time, by which we lost numbers of our
best recruits. The man is generous, perfectly
good-natured, and no doubt brave; but weak
and vain to an extreme degree. You should
keep such people at home, they are excellent
for a court parade. I wish Mrs. Tryon would
send for him."

NOTE.—The following is the Act of the Legislature in regard
to the Regulators. It was an exceedingly harsh measure, but
it was the Act of North Carolinians themselves, and not of the
British Crown or Parliament. So far from being the latter, as
soon as it reached England it was repudiated and denounced,
and similar legislation was forever forbidden ; so that, as is
urged in the text, it was not "British" oppression against
which the Regulators contended :

*An Act for preventing Tumults and Riotous Assemblies, for
the more speedy and effectual punishing the Rioters and for
restoring and preserving the Public Peace of this Province,*

Whereas of late many seditious Riots and tumults have been
in divers Parts of this Province to the disturbance of the Public

Peace, the Obstruction of the Course of Justice, and tending to subvert the Constitution, and the same are yet continued and fomented by Persons disaffected to his Majesty's government. And whereas it hath been doubted by some how far the Laws now in Force are sufficient to inflict punishment adequate to such heinous Offences.

Be it therefore enacted by the Governor, Councill and Assembly, and by the Authority of the same, That if any Persons to the number of ten or more, being unlawfully and tumultuously and riotously assembled together, to the disturbance of the Public Peace, at any time after the first Day of February next, and being openly required or commanded by any one or more Justices of the Peace or Sheriff to disperse themselves, and peaceably to depart to their habitations, shall to the number of ten or more, notwithstanding such Command or Request made remain or continue together by the space of one Hour after such Command or request, that their continuing together to the number of ten or more shall be adjudged Felony, and the offenders therein and each of them, shall be adjudged Felons and shall suffer Death as in case of Felony and shall be utterly excluded from his or their clergy, if found guilty by a verdict of a Jury or shall confess the same, upon his or their arraignment or will not answer directly to the same, according to the Laws of this Province, or shall stand mute or shall be outlawed, and every such Justice of the Peace and Sheriff within the limits of their respective Jurisdictions, are hereby authorized, impowered and required on Notice or Knowledge of any such unlawful, riotous and tumultuous Assembly to resort to the Place where such unlawful riotous, and tumultuous Assembly shall be, of Persons to the Number of ten or more and there to make, or cause to be made such Request or Command.

And be it further enacted by the authority aforesaid that if such Persons so unlawfully, riotously and tumultuously assembled or ten or more of them, after such Request or Command made in manner aforesaid shall continue together and not disperse themselves within one Hour, that then it shall and may be lawful to and for every Justice of the Peace or Sheriff of the County where such Assembly shall be and also to and for such

Person or Persons as shall be commanded to the aiding and assisting to any such Justice of the Peace or Sheriff, who are hereby authorized, impowered and required to command of His Majesty's Subjects of this Province of Age and Ability to be assisting to them therein, to seize and apprehend such Persons so unlawfully, riotously and tumultuously continuing together, after such Request or Command made as aforesaid and forthwith to carry the persons so apprehended before one or more of his Majesty's Justices of the Peace of the County where such Persons shall be so apprehended in Order to their being proceeded against for such their Offences according to Law. And that if the Persons so unlawfully riotously and tumultuously assembled or any of them shall happen to be killed maimed or hurt in the dispersing, seizing or apprehending or endeavoring to disperse, seize or apprehend them by Reason of their resistance that then every such justice of the Peace, Sheriff under Sheriff and all other Persons being aiding or assisting to them or any of them shall be free discharged and indemnified, as well against the King, his Heirs and Successors as against all and every other Person and Persons of for and concerning the killing, maiming or hurting of any such Person or Persons so unlawfully riotously and tumultuously assembled.

And be it further enacted by the authority aforesaid that if any Persons to the Number of Ten or more, unlawfully, riotously or tumultuously assembled together to the disturbance of the public Peace, shall unlawfully and with Force at any time after the first Day of March next, during the sitting of any of the Courts of Judicature within the Province, with an intention to destruct or disturb the proceedings of such Court, assault, beat or wound or openly threaten to assault, beat or wound any of the Judges, Justices or other Officer of such Court, during the continuance of the term or shall assault, beat or wound or openly threaten to assault, beat or wound, or shall unlawfully and with force hinder and destruct any Sheriff, Under Sheriff, Coroner or Collector of the public Taxes in the discharge or execution of his or their office or shall unlawfully and with Force demolish, pull down or destroy or begin to demolish, pull down or destroy any Church or Chapel or any Building for religious Worship o any Court House or Prison or any Dwelling House, Barn Stable or other Outhouse that then every such offence shall be adjudged Felony. And the Offenders therein their leaders abettors and Advisers shall be adjudged felons and shall suffer death as in due case of felony and be utterly excluded from his or their clergy, if found guilty by verdict of a Jury or shall confess the same upon his or their arraignment or will not answer directly to the same according to the laws of this Province or shall stand mute or shall be out-lawed.

And whereas it hath been found by experience that there is great difficulty in bringing to justice Persons who have been or may be guilty of any of the Offences before mentioned : For Remedy thereof, Be it enacted by the Authority aforesaid that it shall and may be lawful to and for the Attorney General of this Province for the time being or his deputies to commence Prosecutions against any Person or Persons who have any time since the first Day of March last or shall at any time hereafter commit or perpetrate any of the Crimes or Offences herein before mentioned in any Superior Court with this Province or in any Court of Oyer and Terminer by the Governor or Commander in Chief for the time being, specially instituted and appointed and the Judges or Justices of such Court are hereby authorized, impowered and required to take Cognizance of all such Crimes and Offences, and proceed to give Judgment and award Execution thereon, although in a different County or District from that wherein the Crime was committed and that all Proceedings thereupon shall be deemed equally valid and sufficient in Law as if the same had been prosecuted in the County or District wherein the Offence was committed, any Law, Usage or Custom to the Contrary notwithstanding.

And be it further enacted, by the Authority aforesaid that the Judges or Justices of such Court of Oyer and Terminer so commissioned shall direct the Clerk of the District wherein such Court of Oyer and Terminer is to be held to issue Writs of Venire Facias, and the proceedings thereon to be in all respects the same as directed by an Act of Assembly passed at New Bern in January in the year of our Lord One thousand

seven hundred and sixty eight intituled An Act for dividing
this Province into six several districts and for establishing a
superior Court of Justice in each of the said districts and regulating the proceedings therein, and for providing adequate
salaries for the Chief Justice and the Associate Justices of the
said superior Courts.

Provided nevertheless that no Person or Persons heretofore
guilty of any of the Crimes or Offences in this Act beforemen-
tioned although convicted thereof in a different County or
district from that wherein such Offence was committed shall
be subject to any other or greater punishment than he or they
would or might have been had this Act never been made.

And to the end that the Justice of the Province be not eluded
by the resistance or escape of such enormous Offenders, Be it
further enacted by the Authority aforesaid, that from and after
the passing of this Act, if any Bill or Bills of any indictment
be found or presentment or presentments made against any
Person or Persons for any of the Crimes or Offences herein
before mentioned it shall and may be Lawful for the Judges
or Justices of the Supreme Court or Court of Oyer and Terminer, wherein such Indictment shall be found or presentment
made and they are hereby impowered and required to issue
their proclamation to be affixed or put up at the Court House
and each Church and Chappel of the County where the Crime
was committed, commanding the Person or Persons against
whom such Bill of Indictment is found or presentment made
to surrender himself or themselves to the Sheriff of the County
wherein such Court is held within sixty Days. And in case
such Person or Persons do not surrender himself or themselves
accordingly, he or they shall be deemed guilty of the offence
charged in the Indictment found or presentment made in like
manner as if he or they had been arraigned and convicted
thereof by due Course of Law, And it shall and may be lawful
to and for any Person or Persons to kill and destroy such
Offenders, and such Person or Persons killing such Offender
or Offenders shall be free discharged and indemnified, as well
against the King, his Heirs and successors, as against all and
every Person and Persons for and concerning the killing and
destroying such Offender or Offenders and the lands and

chattels of such Offender or Offenders shall be forfeited to his Majesty, his Heirs and successors, to be sold by the Sheriff, for the best Price that may be had, at public Vendue, after notice by advertisement ten Days and the Monies arising from such sale, to be paid to the Treasurer of the District wherein the same shall be sold and applied towards defraying the contingent Charges of government.

And whereas by the late Riots and Insurrections at the last Superior Court held for the district of Hillsborough it may be justly apprehended that some endeavors will be made to protect those who have been guilty of such Riots and Insurrections as well as those who may hereafter be guilty of the Crimes and Offences herein before mentioned : For Prevention thereof and restoring Peace and Stability to the regular government of this Province, Be it enacted by the Authority aforesaid, that the Governor or Commander in Chief for the time being is hereby fully authorized and empowered to order and command that necessary draughts be made from the different Regiments of Militia in this Province to be under the Command of such Officer or Officers as he may think proper to appoint for that purpose at the Public Expence to be by him employed in Aid and Assistance of the Execution of this Law, as well as to protect the Sheriffs and Collectors of the public Revenue in Discharge of their several duties, which draught or Detachments of Officers and Soldiers when made shall be found, provided for, and paid, in the same manner and at the same rates and subject to the same Rules and Discipline as directed in case of an Insurrection in and by an Act of Assembly made in the year of our Lord One thousand seven hundred and sixty eight, entitled, An Act for the establishing a Militia in this Province.

And for effectually carrying into execution the purposes aforesaid, Be it enacted by the Authority aforesaid, that it shall and may be Lawful for the Governor and Commander in Chief for the time being to draw upon both or either of the Publick Treasurers of this Province by Warrant from under his Hand and Seal, for Payment of any such sums of Money as shall or may be immediately necessary for the carrying on and performing of such Service and the said Treasurers or either of them are hereby directed and required to answer and pay such

Warrants as aforesaid out of the contingent Fund, which shall be allowed in their settlement of the Public Accounts.

And be it further Enacted by the Authority aforesaid, that if any number of Men shall be found embodied and in an armed and hostile Manner, to withstand or oppose any military Forces, raised in Virtue of this Act, and shall when openly and publickly required, commanded by any Justice of the Peace or Sheriff of the County where the same shall happen, to lay down their Arms and surrender themselves, and then and in such Case the said Persons so unlawfully assembled and withstanding, opposing and resisting shall be considered as Traitors and may be treated accordingly.

And be it further Enacted by the Authority aforesaid, that the Justices of every Superior Court shall cause this Act to be read at the Court House Door, the second Day of each Court for their Counties, and that the Minister, Clerk or Reader of every Parish in this Province shall read or cause the same to be read at every Church, Chappel or other Place of Public Worship within their respective Parishes, once in three Months at least immediately after Divine Service, during the continuance of this Act.

And be it enacted, by the authority aforesaid that this act shall continue and be in Force for one year and no longer.

Read three times in open Assembly and Ratified the 15th Day of January 1771.

WILLIAM TRYON,

JAMES HASELL,

President.

RICHARD CASWELL,

Speaker.

A true Copy of An Act passed last Session of Assembly.

ROBERT PALMER,

Secretary.

CHAPTER V.

The Social Life of the Colony—Marriage of General Waddell—
His Civil Services—Family—Death—Will—Conclusion of
Biography.

THERE is, to the curious in such matters,
a mine of the most interesting information
hidden in the musty records of the oldest
counties in North Carolina, and until these
records shall have been exhausted—and as yet
they have hardly been tapped—there will be
no perfect portrait of the early civilization of
the State.

The minute books of the Courts, of which
tribunals there were at different times various
sorts with curious and conflicting jurisdictions,
and the records of wills and deeds in the
Clerks' and Registers' offices, present the most
attractive field of investigation; and these,
with the private correspondence and traditions
which have been preserved in many families,
afford the best if not the only accurate picture
of the social life and customs of the people.

Some of these customs lingered long after
the beginning of the present century, and in

some parts of the State had not totally disappeared by the middle of it. Especially was this true of the Scotch element of the population, who settled on and near the upper Cape Fear river, and some of whose customs are still preserved in a more or less modified form by their descendants. The settlers who came to the Colony from Ireland were themselves of Scotch descent or birth, and were known as Scotch-Irish. The Rowans, whose name was pronounced Roan, came originally from Lanarkshire in Scotland, as did the ancestors of General Waddell, and it was, doubtless, through the connection or association of these families and that of Dobbs that young Waddell was induced to come to North Carolina.

The social life was a reflex of that in the old country, and to the miserable libels which, under the name of history, have been published concerning the civilization of the Colony, it is only necessary to give for answer the names and attainments of some of the leading spirits who lived in it. From a glance at them it will plainly appear that, so far from being the rude—much less the ignorant and degraded—society sometimes represented, they were, in proportion to population, equal in social and intellectual culture to and as much

attached to the principles of enlightened liberty
as any people on the continent. Many of them
were educated in English universities, or at
Edinboro or Dublin, and owned large estates
where they dispensed a generous and elegant
hospitality. In the Northern end of the
Colony, "the Court end of the Province," in
and around Edenton, "there was," says McRee
in his *Life and Correspondence of James Iredell*,
"in proportion to its population, a greater
number of men eminent for ability, virtue and
erudition than in any other part of America,"
and he gives a long list of names with a brief
biographical notice of each in proof of his
assertion.* This list includes John Harvey,
who was unquestionably a man of great intellectual endowments, and who, but for his death
in 1775, would have been a great leader among
the statesmen of the Revolution; Joseph
Hewes, one of the signers of the Declaration
of Independence; Samuel Johnston, a great
lawyer, Governor of the State and the first
Senator from North Carolina in 1789; Colonel
John Dawson, a lawyer, whose mansion, "Eden
House," was the resort of a "refined society,"
and the seat of a "splendid hospitality," as

---

*Vol. I, 33.

testified to by Mr. Avery (who was himself a
graduate of Princeton, was a signer of the
Mecklenburg Declaration, and Attorney General of the State); Colonel Edward Buncombe,
an educated English gentleman of large wealth,
who was Colonel of the 5th Regiment of North
Carolina Troops, and killed at Germantown
1777; Thomas Jones, a distinguished lawyer,
who drafted the State Constitution in 1776;
Sir Nathaniel Dukinfield, a member of the
Council—and many others, professional men,
merchants and planters, to whom is to be
added James Iredell, the great lawyer, who was
afterwards a Justice of the Supreme Court of
the United States.

In the Southern end of the Province, at
Brunswick and Wilmington, and along the
Cape Fear, there was an equally refined and
cultivated society and some very remarkable
men. No better society existed in America,
and it is but simple truth to say that for clas-
sical learning, wit, oratory, and varied accom-
plishments no generation of their successors
has equalled them.

Their hospitality was boundless and pro-
verbial, and of the manner in which it was
enjoyed there can be no counterpart in the
present age. Some of them had town resi-

dences, but most of them lived on their plantations, and they were not the thriftless characters that by some means it became fashionable
to assume that all Southern planters were.
There was much gayety and festivity among
them, and some of them rode hard to hounds,
but as a general rule they looked after their
estates, and kept themselves as well informed
in regard to what was going on in the world
as the limited means of communication allowed.
There was little display, but in almost every
house could be found valuable plate, and, in
some, excellent libraries. The usual mode of
travel was on horseback, and in "gigs" or
"chairs," which were vehicles without springs
but hung on heavy straps, and to which one
horse, and sometimes, by young beaux, two
horses *tandem* were driven ; a mounted servant
rode behind, or, if the gig was occupied by
ladies, beside the horse. The family coach
was mounted by three steps, and had great
carved leather springs, with baggage rack
behind, and a high, narrow driver's seat and
box in front. The gentlemen wore clubbed
and powdered queues and knee-breeches, with
buckled low-quartered shoes, and many carried
gold or silver snuff-boxes which, being first
tapped, were handed with grave courtesy

13

to their acquaintances when passing the
compliments of the day. There are persons still living who remember seeing these
things in their early youth. The writer of
these lines himself remembers seeing in his
childhood the decaying remains of old "chairs"
and family coaches, and knew at that time
several old negroes who had been body servants in their youth to the proprietors of these
ancient vehicles. It is no wonder they sometimes drove the coaches four-in-hand. It was
not only grand style, but the weight of the
vehicle and the character of the roads made it
necessary.

During the period embraced in these pages,
four-wheeled pleasure vehicles were rare, and
even two-wheeled ones were not common,
except among the town nabobs and well-to-do
planters. The coaches, or chariots, as a certain
class of vehicles was called, were all imported
from England, and the possession of such a
means of locomotion was evidence of high
social position. It was less than twenty years
before the period named, that the first stage
wagon in the Colonies, in 1738, was run from
Trenton to New Brunswick, in New Jersey,
twice a week, and the advertisement of it
assured the public that it would be "fitted up

with benches and covered over so that passen-
gers may sit easy and dry."*

The inns, ordinaries, or taverns, as they
were called before the word *hotel* was borrowed
from the French, were few and far between,
and were of the most primitive kind, and the
consequence was, that every man of substance
kept open house and entertained any respectable traveller, as a matter of course, without
charge.   There was not enough travel to make
it burdensome, and the occasional travellers
were to their hosts what the newspapers of
to-day are to their descendants; and the information imparted by them and the pleasure of
their company, if they were intelligent, supplied the place of the currency which was
generally requisite to every traveller in other
parts of the country when seeking "entertainment for man and beast."   These mere
travellers seldom passed through the back settlements, but only along or near the seacoast,
as that was the most populous and wealthy
region of the country, but if they did wander
farther into the interior the hospitality was as
cordial, if less elegant in its surroundings.
This characteristic of the people of North

*Edward Eggleston in *Century Magazine* for August, 1885.

Carolina marks them as distinctly now as it did then, but, thanks to railroads and modern civilization, they are not required to manifest it in the same way.

As the Northern Colonies soon became populous and their commercial and manufacturing interests became dominant, there was a corresponding change in their social customs; but in the South, which has always been the land of the planter, the conditions, until a very recent period, were little varied, and the social life of the people remained much the same. It was, necessarily, for the most part, a simple and unpretending life, in which the cardinal virtues were cultivated, and it was, in some respects, *sui generis*. It bred pure women and brave men who did not measure the merits of others, or their own, by the extent of their worldly possessions, and did not recognize the golden calf as an object of worship.

It was a life given to hospitality, and, although marked by some features which appear rude and unattractive to modern eyes, was characterized by others which might be imitated with profit by the present generation. The respect for authority, the deference paid to age, to parents, and to women, and the sense of personal honor among men which prevailed, would be regarded as quite fantastic in this age of superior enlightenment; but they are, after all, the truest signs of real civilization and the safest guarantees of good government.

There seems to have been, from a very early period, a decided taste for the drama in Wilmington, which was one of the many evidences of culture among the people. Indeed, the first drama ever written in America was written there in 1759 by a young man named Thomas Godfrey, a native of Philadelphia, who died in Wilmington August 3d, 1763, aged 27, and is buried in St. James's church-yard. His father, of the same name, in 1730, made the improvement on Davis's quadrant, for which the Royal Society granted him £200.

Young Godfrey's tragedy was entitled "A Prince of Parthia." It was, with some of the author's poems, edited by Nathaniel Evans, and published in Philadelphia in 1765. It gave much promise, but the early death of the author dashed the hopes of his friends. In Tyler's "History of American Literature," it is thus spoken of: "The whole drama is powerful in diction and in action; the characters are firmly and consistently developed; there are scenes of pathos and tragic vividness; the plot advances with rapid movement and with culminating force."

Doubtless, during the sessions of the Legislature "A Prince of Parthia" was put on the boards by the amateurs of Wilmington and greeted with thunders of applause. There were, however, some professional actors of distinction who played there in those days. In an interesting letter to the Bishop of London, dated June 11th, 1768, Governor Tryon speaks of a talented young actor, named Giffard, who applied to him for recommendation to the Bishop "for ordination orders, he having been invited by some principal gentlemen of the Province to be inducted into a parish, and to set up a school for the education of youth." Tryon said the young man had assured him that it was no sudden caprice that induced him to make the application, but that it was the result of very mature deliberation—"that he was most wearied of the vague life of his present profession, and fully persuaded he could employ his talents to more benefit to society by going into holy orders and superintending the education of the youth in this Province." Tryon also expressed a doubt whether the Bishop would choose to take a member of the theatre into the church, but testified to the young man's excellent conduct, and concluded his letter with the following remark: "If your Lordship grants Mr. Giffard his petition, you will take off the best player on the American stage." Mr. Giffard took Tryon's letter to London, going by way of Providence, where he was under contract to play, but whether he succeeded in his wish to enter the ministry, or ever returned to North Carolina or not, we do not know.

The country which these North Carolina Colonists inhabited was one of the most inviting regions for settlers in America. The climate was mild, the soil adapted to the production of every cereal and plant necessary or useful to man; the forests vast, filled with game of every kind and fragrant with the odors of a thousand different kinds of herbs and flowers; the rivers were numerous, some of them magnificent, and all teeming with fish and swarming with wild fowl. Thus all the conditions required for the most generous display of plantation hospitality were present, or attainable with the least effort, and the consequence was that a social life, in many respects the most charming and peculiar that has perhaps ever existed, was developed and continued to flourish until trampled out of existence by the iron heel of war.

It was while enjoying the pleasures of this social life during an interval in his military service, and while attending the session of the Assembly at Wilmington, that General Waddell met the lady who became his wife. She was Mary Haynes, daughter of Captain Roger Haynes, and granddaughter of Rev. Richard Marsden, the first Rector of St. James's Parish, in Wilmington. Of Captain Haynes very little is known beyond the fact that he was in the British service. He lived at Castle Haynes,* about nine miles North of Wilmington, on the Northeast branch of Cape Fear— which plantation adjoined the Hermitage where Mr. Marsden lived—and he had died previous to 1753. The marriage of General Waddell took place at Castle Haynes sometime in the year 1762.

The only other daughter of Captain Haynes, Margaret, was married some years previously to John Burgwin, Esq., who was, for a time, the Treasurer of the Southern part of the Province. Not long after General Waddell's marriage he joined Mr. Burgwin in business in Wilmington, the firm being John Burgwin & Co., with branch establishments in various

---

*This place is commonly called Castle *Hayne*, and the Railroad Station there is so labelled.

places in the back country. The business was managed by Mr. Burgwin, who was educated to mercantile life in England, General Waddell, when not engaged on frontier duty or in the Legislature, passing most of his time in visiting and superintending his different estates, of which there were four or five. His principal residence was at Bellefont, in Bladen County, generally called "the Waddell place," which is situate about two miles below Elizabethtown, and is interesting as containing the grave of the distinguished Lieutenant Colonel Webster, Lord Cornwallis's favorite officer, who was mortally wounded at Guilford Court House in 1781.* There he lived for some years dispensing a most generous hospitality and enjoying the unbounded respect and confidence of the people.

As he had previously, in 1757 and 1760, been a magistrate and member of Assembly from Rowan County, so in 1762 he was appointed a Justice of the Peace, and elected to the Assembly from Bladen. He was also one

---

*In 1810, when a party of gentlemen, including Judge Toomer and Hon. Alfred Moore, went to Bellefont to remove the remains of Judge Alfred Moore, they inquired for the spot where Webster was buried. An aged slave named Lisburn, who had belonged to General Waddell, and was named after his birth-place in Ireland, pointed it out to them, he having

of the Justices who presided over the Inferior Court of New Hanover County in 1764, and in that year the County of Brunswick was established out of the territory of New Hanover and Bladen, which explains his being in command of the Brunswick militia in the ensuing year when the Stamp Act troubles occurred. The record does not show his presence in the Court more than once or twice, nor does it show that the sessions of that Court, which met every three months, were interrupted by the Stamp Act excitement; but on the record of the *Superior* Court for April, 1766, there is the following entry:

The actions for trial at April Term, 1766, were all continued over for October Term on acc't of the Stamp Act.

In 1768 he went on a visit to England and Ireland, and while there sat for his portrait to a distinguished artist, who made a beautiful miniature likeness of him on ivory. From this miniature, which is the only picture ever taken of him, the engraving in the front of this

witnessed Webster's funeral. The grave was opened, and, upon removing the decayed lid of the coffin, there lay the British hero, perfect for an instant in sight of all, but in a moment there was only a handful of brown dust.—*Statement of Hon. Jno. D. Toomer and Hon. A. Moore.*

volume is taken. It is believed to be the work of Gainesborough.

Until the passage of the Stamp Act, as has already appeared, General Waddell had been a staunch and steady friend of the government, and one of its well-tried and most faithful servants, notwithstanding the annoying and irritating acts of the unfortunate and unhappy Governor Dobbs, but after that event there was an evident lack of zeal in his loyalty, although there was, as yet, no talk of *independence* anywhere in America. He was again a member of the Assembly in 1765, when Governor Tryon prorogued the body to prevent them from sending delegates to the Stamp Act Congress, but although prevented from acting in his legislative capacity on the subject, he was, as heretofore described, one of the most active leaders of the popular movement against it, both in the meetings which passed resolutions in Wilmington and the armed resistance at Brunswick. He was again a member in 1766 and in 1771, after the Regulators' war was over. He owned lands in Rowan, Anson, Bladen and New Hanover, but Bladen was the only County in which he permanently resided.

It seemed to have been no unusual thing in those days for a man to live in one county and serve as a representative from another, just as it is possible, though not usual now, for a member of Congress to live in one district and be elected from another in the same State.

No record of any of the debates in the Colonial Assembly was kept, and only the necessary minutes of the sessions were preserved.

From these General Waddell appears to have been recognized as a prominent member, as he was nearly always, put upon important committees; but the probability is, that he was rather a "business" member than a speaker.

It was the general supposition that he was a member of the Council either during Dobbs's or Tryon's administration, or both; but the records only show that he was recommended to the Crown by Dobbs in 1762, and Tryon in 1771, for that position.

In his letter to Lord Hillsborough, dated Newbern, 28th January, 1771, Tryon, after nominating Colonel Hugh Waddell, Mr. Marmaduke Jones, and Sir Nathaniel Dukenfield, uses the following language:

Colonel Waddell had the honor to see your Lordship about two years· since in England. He honorably distinguished himself last war while he commanded the Provincials of this province against· the Cherokee Indians, possesses an easy fortune, and is in much esteem as a gentleman of honor and spirit. He has, I confess, endeared himself to my friendship by the generous offer he made me but last week of his voluntary services against the insurgents of this province.

He does not seem to have received the appointment. The Council were appointed by the Crown upon the recommendation of the Governor, and the members of Assembly were elected by the people. The fact that even while on military duty he was often chosen by them as a representative, and was kept, almost up to the day of his death, alternating between service on the frontier and in the Assembly, is the strongest evidence that he held a high place in their esteem and confidence. Indeed, he was both a trusted officer of the government, and a universally recognized leader of the people almost from the beginning of his career to its close—an exceptional distinction which justifies the eulogiums which have been pronounced upon him in the pages of every North Carolina writer who has discussed the period in which he lived, although very few of the details of his public service or private life have been preserved.

In the Fall of 1772 he was contemplating another visit to England, and, according to a family tradition, had gone to Fort Johnston, at the mouth of the Cape Fear, to take ship for the voyage, when he was seized with the illness that resulted in his death. The same tradition says this illness was caused by sleeping in damp sheets. Whatever the cause the sickness was of long duration, for in his will, which was made on the 10th day of November, 1772, he says: "I, Hugh Waddell, of the County of Bladen, and Province of North Carolina, being sick and weak," &c., and he did not die until the 9th day of April following, nearly five months afterward.

He was, at the time of his death, in the 39th year of his age, and, therefore, the references to him in the various histories of the State as "the old General," "the brave old veteran," and the like, furnish a good illustration of the natural but sometimes amusingly incorrect habit of designating persons of a long-past generation as "old," although it is readily accounted for in his case, by the fact that he had been longer in the military service, and was better known as a soldier than any person in the Province previous to the Revolution.

He was buried at Castle Haynes, which estate came to him through his wife, and she was buried there three or four years afterwards.

In his will, which disposed of a large estate in lands in Rowan, Bladen and New Hanover

Counties, and in slaves, town lots, "goods and profits in trade," plate, &c., &c., there is no mention made of any relative besides his wife and children, except his "sister Hannah, of the County of Down in the North of Ireland," to whom he bequeathed one hundred guineas. He had other relatives, more or less near, residing in Ireland, however, and their descendants now reside in and about Lisburn, from which place he came.

"The blind preacher" of Virginia, to whom reference has already been made as having come from the same part of Ireland about the same time, was near the same age as the General, and the two well illustrated, though in different spheres, the race to which they belonged, which for piety and pugnacity is *facile princeps* among the nations of the earth. Each was an agent of civilization, and both died with the consciousness of duty faithfully done, leaving to their posterity an honorable name and fame.

General Waddell, by his marriage, had three sons, Haynes, Hugh and John. They were sent to England to be educated after his death, and the oldest, Haynes, having contracted an illness from hunting in the Fens of Lincolnshire, died on his return voyage to America in 1784, and was buried at sea. He was not of age, as appears by a recital in a deed from his brothers.

The two surviving sons, Hugh and John, divided one of the largest estates on the Cape Fear, and each by his subsequent marriage received a large addition to his property. Hugh married, first, Miss Heron, by whom he had one daughter, Mrs. John Swann, and next the daughter of Judge Alfred Moore, by whom he had a large family. John married the only daughter, and only child, of General Francis Nash, who was killed at the battle of Germantown in 1777. They both became planters on the Cape Fear and continued so all their lives. Hugh died at Bellefont in 1827, and John at Pittsboro in 1830. They took no part in public affairs, but commanded the respect and good will of all who knew them by practicing the sweet charities of life. The former was universally recognized as the Uncle Toby of his generation, and the latter as a model country gentleman.

More than a year and a half had elapsed after the Regulators' war before General Waddell was attacked by the disease which finally killed him, and during that period the idea of separation from Great Britain took root in the Colonies and began to grow with great rapidity throughout the whole of America. When Josiah Quincey, of Boston, visited the Cape Fear country in the Spring of 1773, and enjoyed so much the hospitality extended to him by the "best company," as related in his Memoirs, and while "the plan of Continental correspondence, highly relished, much wished for, and resolved upon as proper to be pursued " by his hosts, was being hatched, General Waddell was on his death-bed; otherwise he would have been very sure, like his intimate friends who were present, to have taken a part in those deliberations.

That he would, if he had lived, have been an active and prominent leader in the Revolution—certainly the most prominent North Carolina soldier—admits of no doubt. All his friends and associates on the Cape Fear, as well as his comrades before and at the time of the Regulators' outbreak, were among the first to take up arms; and, being like-minded with them in regard to the rights of the Colonies, his military experience and soldierly qualities would have marked him at once as the most fitting person in North Carolina for military command, while his acquaintance and former service with General Washington would have secured the confidence of the Commander-in-

Chief from the outset. The State suffered a great loss in his premature death at that critical period.

In reviewing his life and reflecting upon the events amidst which it was passed, one must be impressed with a sense of the services rendered to their country and to posterity by the men who then inhabited the Colonies. It is hardly possible for us of the present generation to fully appreciate the nature and importance of those services. How difficult, for instance, would it be in these days of telegraphs, railroads, breech-loading arms, pontoon trains, and the like, to appreciate thoroughly the trials and dangers accompanying the expedition from middle North Carolina through that terrible mountain wilderness to Tennessee, or that one to Pittsburg, Pennsylvania (Fort Du Quesne), on foot, without quartermaster or commissary stores, artillery or camp equipage, and armed with flint-lock muskets, which a heavy rain might render useless; and this, too, through a hostile region swarming with merciless savages, from whom at every mountain pass or covert, at every hour, day or night, an attack might be expected! The North Carolina troops at Fort Loudon and Fort Du Quesne were actually farther from home than they would be to-day if in Mexico or Europe.

And if we turn from the physical trials by which they were beset, to the moral problems which confronted them, our respect and admiration for them is only increased. The difficulties constantly arising in the administration of their local affairs, the perpetual conflicts with exacting and tyrannical Royal Governors, and the increasing encroachments by the Crown and Parliament of Great Britain upon their inherited and chartered rights as British subjects, which finally drove them into armed rebellion, were all met and overcome with the same heroic spirit.

It is an old story, and one that has often burned on eloquent lips and been pictured by the brush of the literary artist, but for the patriot and student of history it can never cease to have a profound interest, for it reproduces for his contemplation an era full of valuable lessons.

CHAPTER VI.

A Historical Sketch of the Former Town of Brunswick, on the Cape Fear River.

IN Clarendon's History of the Rebellion, the following passage occurs:

There had been, some months before, a design of Prince Rupert upon the city of Bristol, by correspondence with some of the chief inhabitants of the city, who were weary of the tyranny of Parliament; but it had been so unskilfully or unhappily carried that when the Prince was near the town, with such a party of horse and foot as he made choice of, it was discovered, and many principal citizens apprehended by Nathaniel Fiennes, son of the Lord Say, and then Governor of that city for the Parliament. At this time special direction and order was sent thither "that he should, with all severity and expedition, proceed against those conspirators (as they called them); and, thereupon, by a sentence and judgment of a council of war, Alderman Yeomans, who had been High Sheriff of the city, and of great reputation in it, and George Bouchier, another citizen of principal account, were (against all interposition his Majesty could make) both hanged."*

*Vol. I, page 389, Oxford Edition, 1843.

The time at which this event occurred was in the year 1643, and this was the fate of the loyalist leader Yeomans.

Two years previous thereto the quickly-suppressed, but bloody *Irish* rebellion had broken out, and Hume, in his history, thus speaks of one of the instigators of that enterprise:

A gentleman, called Roger Moore, much celebrated among his countrymen for valor and capacity, formed the project of expelling the English, and engaged all the heads of the native Irish in the conspiracy, especially Sir Phelim O'Neale, the representative of the Tyrone family, and Lord Maguire.

Unable to control the fury of the Irish, who began a general massacre, and horrified by their atrocities, Moore fled from the country and went to Flanders.

Upon the restoration of Charles II, in recognition of his father's services, the oldest son of Robert Yeomans (or Yeamans, as he spelled it), who had gone to seek his fortune in Barbadoes, was knighted by the King and became Sir John Yeamans. He, with other gentlemen there, sent, in 1663, an expedition under Hilton to explore the Cape Fear River, on which a Massachusetts colony had made (but soon abandoned) a settlement in 1660. Upon the return of the expedition with a glowing account of the country, Sir John Yeamans brought over a colony, and in 1665 settled it upon the site of the former one at the mouth of Town Creek, eight miles below Wilmington, on the west bank of the river. He received from the Lords Proprietors a grant for thirty-two miles square, and was made the Governor of the colony. He remained there six years, and, in 1671, was made Governor of "Carteret County," as South Carolina was then called, to which place he went, taking his colony with him, and soon after founded Charleston, which was the name of the settlement he had left on Town Creek.

While residing there, James Moore, the grandson of the rebel Roger Moore, who had also come to America to seek his fortune, married the daughter of Yeamans, thus uniting the blood of the English loyalist and Irish rebel, and afterwards was also Governor of South Carolina.

The younger son of Governor James Moore, Maurice Moore, having come with his brother, Colonel James Moore, to suppress the Indian outbreaks in North Carolina in 1711, concluded that he would re-settle the Cape Fear, which had remained unoccupied ever since his grandfather's colony left it, and accordingly he returned there about 1723, and in 1725 laid out the town of Brunswick, about eight miles below the site of the original settlement, and sixteen miles below Wilmington. Two of his brothers, Roger and Nathaniel, came with him, as did many others.

How it was laid out is told in an Act of the Assembly of North Carolina, passed at the session which began on the 20th April, 1745 (old style). The Act was entitled "An Act to encourage persons to settle in the town of Brunswick, on the Southwest side of Cape Fear River," and the preamble sets forth the fact that Maurice Moore, Esq., then deceased, had given 320 acres of land on the Southwest side of Cape Fear for a town called Brunswick (in 1725), and that "the Hon. Roger Moore, Esq.," in order to make the town more regular, had added another parcel of land to it; that a great part of said lands was laid out in lots of a half acre each, many of which were taken up and good houses built thereon; and proper places were appointed by Maurice Moore for a church, court-house, burying-place, market house, and other public buildings; that confusion had arisen about some of the titles to the unsold part, which it was desirable to

settle, etc. "And whereas, the trade of Cape
Fear River consists in naval stores, rice and
lumber, commodities of great bulk and small
value, all due encouragement ought to be
given to large ships to come into the said river
to take off the said commodities; and as all
large ships which come into the said river are
obliged to lie at Brunswick, and that town, for
the want of a sufficient number of inhabitants,
and by reason of the easy navigation thereto,
is much exposed to the invasion of foreign
enemies in time of war, and pirates in time of
peace, therefore we pray your most sacred
Majesty that it may be enacted," &c.

The last lines of the above preamble set
forth facts, the truth of which was amply justified by the depth of water marked on Wim-
ble's map of the mouth of the Cape Fear, made
in 1738, and by the raids of the two pirates,
Richard Worley and Steed Bonnet, who were
captured and hanged by Governor Johnson and
William Rhett, in the year 1717;* and these
facts were further justified by the attack of

---

*The Boston *News-Letter* of July 16th, 1724, says that his
Majesty's ship "Station," captured and carried into Charleston 130 pirates, from whom they took £5,000 as the share of
each of the captors.

a Spanish squadron on the town three years after the passage of the Act.

The town was twenty years old when the Act was passed. It never contained more than four hundred white inhabitants, but there were among these many of the wealthiest, most refined and cultivated people in the Province— the equals in every respect of the best people on the continent—and the reputation of the town for intelligence, public spirit and un-bounded hospitality soon became wide-spread. The fact that, for reasons which will presently be given, the population of Brunswick was eventually absorbed by the younger town of Wilmington (both towns being in New Hanover County until 1764, when Brunswick County was established), will explain the confusion that has appeared sometimes in North Carolina histories in the assignment of a residence to certain distinguished men in both towns, or only in Wilmington.

At March Term, 1727, of the General Court, held at Edenton, the following entry was made :

It being represented to this Court that it is highly necessary that a Ferry should be settled over Cape Fear River, and that part of the Province not being laid out into precincts, therefore it is by this Court ordered, that the

Ferry be kept for that river by Cornelius Harnett, from the place designed for a town on the West side of the river to a place called the Haule-over. And that he receive the sum of five shillings for a man and horse, and half a crown for each person, and that no person to keep any Ferry within ten miles of the said places.

This ferry was reached from the North by the road which passed over the little bridge on Smith's Creek, and thence due South along what is now MacRae Street in Wilmington to the Haul-over nearly opposite Brunswick.

This road to Brunswick, through Wilmington, was at that time the only route from the Northern part of the Province to South Carolina. The only two ferries on the lower Cape Fear were this at Brunswick, and one where Wilmington now is; and this latter was not directly across the river, but from about the foot of the present Dock street, past Point Peter, and four miles up the Northwest branch to MacLaine's Bluff, where the Navassa Factory now stands. The causeway across Eagles's Island was begun by Colonel Wm. Dry in December, 1764, and finished by Governor Benjamin Smith in 1791, under Acts of Assembly.

The Cornelius Harnett named in the Act of

1727, was the father of the distinguished man
of that name, and was either already a resident of Brunswick, or moved there soon after.
It was said that he kept the inn there, and
certain deeds corroborate the statement. His
son was four years old when this order of the
General Court establishing the ferry was made,
and he passed his youth and early manhood in
Brunswick, and very probably was one of those
who helped to drive off the Spaniards and blow
up one of their ships in 1748, as he was then
twenty-five years old. His name is a household word on the Cape Fear, and his career is
a part of the history of the Revolutionary
period. He is regarded, however, as a Wilmington man, because he began to attain distinction after removing there, lived the greater
part of his life there, and died there.

Indeed, that may be said of the majority of
the great men of the lower Cape Fear during
the Revolution, as at that time it was the only
town in that section of the State; but most of
them had previously lived in Brunswick, or
its vicinity. Hooper, the signer of the Declaration of Independence, had not, as he did not
come to North Carolina from Massachusetts
until 1764; but MacLaine and McGuire, each
of whom became Attorney General, and a

number of other distinguished men, moved to Wilmington after Brunswick began to decay. McGuire was a loyalist when the Revolution broke out, and went to England, but the others were all patriots, and some of them became leaders in that struggle. General Robert Howe, one of the most illustrious of these leaders, always lived in or near Brunswick; and so did General James Moore, who commanded the whole Southern Department, and his brother, Judge Maurice Moore, and the latter's son, Judge Alfred Moore, afterwards a Judge of the United States Supreme Court, and some of the distinguished members of the Ashe family, and Governor Benj. Smith and Colonel Wm. Dry, and many others of note.

When the character and fame of these men are considered, and the size of the town is remembered, it may be confidently asserted that no community, so small, on the continent, ever contained at the same time so many men who afterwards became so distinguished as soldiers and jurists and statesmen.

And yet, alas! except in the faintest and most confused way, not only the deeds, but the very names of these heroes and patriots have well-nigh ceased to be remembered, and the place of their abode—once the busy mart, the seat of refined culture and generous hospitality—has long been the home of the fox and the owl. A few grave-stones and the four walls of the old church of St. Philip, surrounded by a tangled thicket, are the only remaining evidences of the existence of the ancient borough.

The old church was built of brick imported from England, and the walls are nearly three feet thick. They are solid still, though scarred and pitted by shot fired in two wars, and will apparently stand for another century. The dense thicket of trees and shrubbery not only incloses the burying-ground and church, but has taken possession of the interior of the church, and trees, several inches in diameter, have sprung out of the tops of the walls. It must have been quite an imposing structure, with its high pitch and three lofty arched doors, and the chancel windows were quite grand. Its dimensions were as follows: length, 76.6; width, 54.3; height of walls now standing, 24.4; number of windows 11, measuring 15 x 7 feet; doors, 3; thickness of walls, 2.9.

During the late war between the States, a heavy earthwork, called Fort Anderson, was constructed between the church and the river, and on the spot where nearly one hundred years before the defiant patriots stood resisting the landing of the stamps.

In digging away the earth for the construction of this work, the laborers found some old coin and other relics. When the fort, after a severe bombardment by the United States fleet, was abandoned, before the fall of Wilmington in 1865, the Northern soldiers occupied it, and the corner-stone of the venerable sanctuary, which had been respected for more than a century, was dug out, and some of the tombs were broken into, probably in a fruitless search for treasure. If the soldier who removed one particular grave-stone could read Latin, and was not utterly insensible, he must have felt a little uncomfortable, especially if he observed that the occupant of that tomb was a youthful bride of seventeen, for on the slab was carved the old curse,

" Quisquis hoc marmor sustulerit
Ultimus suorum moriatur."

In its earliest days, the Legislature used sometimes to meet in Brunswick, and Governor Gabriel Johnstone, of pleasant memory, upon his arrival in October, 1734, took the oaths of office there.

In 1748 the town was attacked by a squad-

ron of Spanish privateers, who had entered the
river and were plundering the country; but
the plucky inhabitants rallied to the defence
of their property and whipped off the invaders,
after blowing up one of their ships and cap-
turing some valuable property. This attack
occurred on the 8th November, 1748—at least
the vessel was blown up on that day—and
among the articles captured was a painting,
an "*Ecce Homo*," which had probably been
stolen from some church or private residence
somewhere on the coast. The captured property was appropriated, by an Act of the Legislature, to the church of St. Philip at Brunswick,
and the church of St. James at Wilmington,
and the "*Ecce Homo*" is still preserved in the
vestry-room of St. James. It is not a fine work
of art, but is an interesting memento of the
gallant exploit of the men of Brunswick. The
pirates continued their work up to a much
later date.*

*There are several privateers on our coast from the West
Indies; they have taken an English ship coming to Cape Fear
with dry goods, and another small vessel, and have turned the
sailors ashore, and we have no sloop to cruise upon the coast.
The *Baltimore*, Captain Hood, which should be stationed at
Cape Fear, was called off in Spring to Nova Scotia, and hitherto when they return in Winter, they look into Cape Fear
and stay some days, but finding no balls or entertainments

It was at Brunswick that George III was proclaimed King in the presence of the Governor (Dobbs), the members of the Council, and a number of the principal inhabitants and planters. An account of the ceremony was given by Governor Dobbs in a letter to the Secretary of the Board of Trade, under date of February 9th, 1761,* as follows:

I sent for such of the Council as were in this neighborhood, and next day, Friday, had his Majesty proclaimed here by all the gentlemen near this place, the militia drawn out and a triple discharge from Fort Johnston of twenty-one guns, and from all the ships in the river; and at the same time sent out an express for the other Councillors in this neighborhood to meet me at Wilmington next day, Saturday the 7th, where his Majesty was again proclaimed by the corporation and gentlemen of the neighborhood, under a triple salute of twenty-one guns, where we had an entertainment prepared; the militia were drawn out, and the evening concluded by bonfires, illuminations, and a ball and supper with all unanimity and demonstrations of joy.

there, they sail away and spend the Winter in Charles Town, under pretence that they can't clean in at Cape Fear, although they may have all conveniences for it.—*Dobbs to Board of Trade, October* 31*st,* 1756.

*Colonial Records, Vol. VI, 520.

He also said that he had sent the proclamation by express to Newbern to be published and forwarded to every county and borough in the Province.

Under date of April 16th, 1761, the Rev. John McDowell, Rector of the Parish of St. Philip—in a long complaining letter to the Secretary of the Society for the Propagation of the Gospel, in which he is severe on his Vestry—writes: "The roof of the new church at Brunswick is fallen down again: it was struck with lightning last July, and afterwards a prodigious and immoderate quantity of rain falling on it made it all tumble down, and there it lies just as it fell; the chapel is a most miserable old house, only twenty-four feet by fifteen, and every shower of rain or blast of wind blows quite through it." The reverend gentleman seemed to be about to quit his charge because of difficulties with his Vestry, who, he said, strove to keep their minister "in the greatest state of subjection and dependence," and wouldn't pay him a sufficient salary, and were, some of them, sadly lacking in piety. He modestly says, "But they will repent their obliging me to leave them, for I have done and would have done more for them than any they have ever had, or, I dare say, ever will have."

15

It would be unfair to the Vestry, however, not
to publish their side of the case, which is contained in the following suggestive letter, dated
Brunswick, 24th March, 1761, and addressed
to the Rector:

The Vestry have taken into consideration
the difficulties you allege in officiating at the
Blue Banks during the two hot and two cold
months, and are content that you be permitted
to exchange the Sundays in July and August,
allotted for that Chapel, with Brunswick for
other Sundays in a more moderate season, you
giving due notice of such exchange; and as to
cold months, we know of none in this country
to prevent one of your healthy constitution
from riding twenty-four miles: indeed, a day
of bad weather may happen now and then, for
which accident all reasonable allowance will
be made, as heretofore has been made. As to
the addition of salary which you insist on, we
cannot but observe that when you agreed to
serve the cure of this Parish on the 5th June,
1758, you thankfully accepted of £100 a year,
when your family was larger than it is now,
and you willingly undertook harder duty than
is now proposed to you.

But now, Sir, his Excellency the Governor
and Vestry, having by their joint recommendation of you, procured £50 sterling a year,
the generous bounty of the Society for the
Propagating the Gospel, you disdain to accept
from our Parish £120 Proclamation money a

year; you discover difficulties in the exercise
of your function which never before occurred,
and you are pleased to insist on such a salary
as they never have given, and such as many
of this Parish, in the present distressed state
of their trade and circumstances, cannot easily
give you.

If you are pleased to continue on the terms
we have now proposed, we shall be glad to
contribute all in our power to make every part
of your duty agreeable to you. We are, Rev.
Sir, your most humble servants.

It was several years before the church was
finished and dedicated, it seems, for the Rev.
John Barnett, writing to the Secretary of the
Society for the Propagation of the Gospel, from
Brunswick on the 11th June, 1768, says that
though he had apprehended great delay in the
finishing the new church, it was then "so
nearly completed as with great decency to
admit of the performance of Divine worship in
it," and proceeds to inform them that, with
the assistance of the Rev. Mr. Wills, of Wilmington, he had dedicated St. Philip's church
on Whit Tuesday. "Being wholly unac-
quainted," he says, "with a proper form or
mode of dedication, I wrote to several clergy-
men for their advice, but not one could give
the least information. I then drew up a form,

which was approved by his Excellency and the Council, and, indeed, gave an universal satisfaction." He also said that the people of the parish so violently opposed the presentation of the Crown to the Living that he thought he would have to leave.

On the 20th September, 1761, according to the *London Magazine* for December of that year, a fearful hurricane swept the coast, lasting from Monday the 20th to Friday the 24th, but raging with most violence on Thursday the 23d. "Many houses," says the account, "were thrown down, and all the vessels, except one, in Cape Fear river driven on shore. It forced open a new channel for that river at a place called the Haul-over, between the Cedar House and the Bald Head.* This new channel was found on soundings to be eighteen feet deep at high water, and is near half a mile wide."

The breach thus made across the sand-strip between the ocean and the river, was afterwards known as New Inlet, and was—until recently closed by the United States Government—as often used by vessels bound to and

---

*Gov. Dobbs says this happened on the 22d. Col. Rec., Vol. VI, 605.

from Wilmington as the main entrance at the
mouth of the river, and was defended during
the late war by Fort Fisher. It is about four
miles below Brunswick, on the opposite side
of the river, which is about two miles wide
along that part of its course. There seem to
have been two places called the Haul-over, one
opposite Brunswick where Harnett's Ferry
was, and that where New Inlet broke through.
Harnett's Ferry was certainly not between
Brunswick and the lower one. If there were
not two, as one tradition says, then the *London Magazine* was in error in calling the place
where New Inlet was the Haul-over.

In a letter to the Lords of the Board of
Trade, written in 1761, Governor Dobbs, answering a question as to the trade of the Province, says: "No foreign trade whatever is
carried on between this colony and any foreign
plantation, except with Eustatia and St. Croix,
and with no foreign countries in Europe except
with the Madeiras and Azores, and with the
Canaries for wine, salt from Portugal not being
allowed to be imported. These are brought
by ships from Britain; nor have we any trade
with Ireland upon account that naval stores,
and other enumerated commodities are pro-
hibited, which is a great help to Britain and

this colony. The natural produce and staple commodities of this Province (for of manufactures there are none) consist of naval stores, masts, yards, plank and ship timber, Indian corn, pease, rice, and of late flour, hemp, flax and flax seed, tobacco, bees and myrtle wax, and some indigo." He gives the number of ships annually coming to the port of Brunswick at ninety, with a tonnage of four thousand eight hundred and thirty, most of them being small, and says that at that time (1761) there were only about fifty ships owned in the colony. His description of the navigation of the Cape Fear shows that the depth of water was greater than it ever was afterwards, until the closing of New Inlet recently, that Inlet not having broken through, as already said, until 22d September, 1761. Upon this subject he says: "But the chief river for navigation and trade is Cape Fear river, there being eighteen feet water upon the bar, navigable for large ships above Brunswick fifteen miles up the river and as high as Wilmington, after passing the flats upon which there is about eleven or twelve feet water (since a new entrance has been opened by a hurricane on the 22d September last at a place called the Haul-over, eight or ten miles above the former entrance), and is navigable for small vessels for above one hundred miles farther up on the Northwest branch, and above sixty miles higher on the Northeast branch, in which a rapid tide flows for near one hundred miles, this being the only inlet for all the Southern and Western parts of this Province."

Governor Dobbs lived in Brunswick, and had a plantation on Town Creek, a few miles above the town, where he was buried. Governor Tryon also lived there, and owned two houses in the town, one of which was approached by a fine cedar avenue, and was called Russellboro: it was bought by him from Governor Dobbs's son, and was the residence formerly occupied by Dobbs. It contained fifty-five acres, and was adjoining the town on the North side.

The town was again visited by a hurricane on the 7th September, 1769, which nearly destroyed it, and which did, on the 9th, destroy Newbern, where six persons were drowned. In truth, the whole existence of the old town was marked by storms, natural and political; and nearly a century after it had ceased to exist, and when the silence and solitude which had so long enveloped it was broken for the first time, it was by the engi-

neer's pick and spade in the construction of a
military work for use in a civil war.

Immediately North of Brunswick, and adjoining the tract on which the town was laid
out, is the celebrated Orton plantation, which
is at the Southern terminus of the rice lands
of the Cape Fear river. It has always been
regarded as one of the most valuable plantations in that part of the State, and is a historic
place. Like most of the valuable lands on or
near the Cape Fear, it was originally granted
(1725)to Colonel Maurice Moore, and was first
settled by his brother Roger, commonly called
"King Roger," who owned immense tracts in
that part of the country. The latter was also
a much-married man. One of his wives was
Catharine Rhett, and his daughter by her was
the mother of Governor Benjamin Smith.

Governor Smith afterwards owned Orton,
and his brother James owned the adjoining
plantation, "Kendall," which had also belonged to King Roger. James Smith was the
father of the late Hon. R. Barnwell Rhett and
his brothers, who took the name of Rhett and
moved to South Carolina. The plantation
next to Kendall was "Lilliput," which was
first granted (1725) to Hon. Eleazar Allen,
Chief Justice of North Carolina, who died in
1738, and whose tombstone, and that of his

wife, is still in a good state of preservation.
Governor Tryon also owned Lilliput in 1768.
King Roger and his family are buried at Orton
plantation beneath a brick mound. This
sobriquet of "King" was given him because
of the state in which he lived, and of the manner in which he had controlled the Indians,
whom he defeated in a fight at the "Sugar
Loaf," a place on the East side of the river
nearly opposite to Orton. One tradition about
him is that he was a mighty hunter, and that
not long before his death, having asked his
eldest son what part of his lands he would
prefer to have, the son replied that as he believed there were "more deer" in a certain
region (mentioning it), he would prefer that.

Orton has, from its original settlement to
this day, been celebrated as the best hunting
and fishing ground in all the lower Cape Fear
country, and among the animals once hunted
there, but which have since disappeared,
was the panther, a specimen of which Governor Tryon sent from Brunswick on the
28th March, 1767, accompanied by the following letter, to the Earl of Sherburne:

As the panther of this continent, I am told,
has never been imported into Europe, and as

it is the king of the American forests, I pre-
sume to send a male panther under your
Lordship's patronage, to be presented for his
Majesty's acceptance.   He is six months old;
I have had him four months; by constantly
handling he is become perfectly tame and
familiar.   When full grown his coat will much
resemble that of the lioness.   Panthers have
been killed (for it is very uncommon to catch
them alive) ten feet in length from the nose to
the end of the tail.   I am very solicitous for
his safe arrival, as I am ambitious that he may
be permitted to add to his Majesty's collection
of wild beasts.

The Orton tract embraces several thousand
acres of pine lands in rear of the rice plantation,
which is a great deer walk, and includes
a very large pond of several miles in length,
which is filled with choice fish—chiefly black
bass and the finest varieties of perch.   Part of
the hunting ground and part of the pond are
really attached to the Kendall tract, but they
are generally spoken of as belonging to Orton.
For more than a hundred years it has been the
resort of sportsmen and the scene of unbounded
hospitality.   Indeed, more than one hundred
and fifty years ago it had an established reputation for generous hospitality, and there is a
record in existence, dated 1734, which proves

it.   It is a pamphlet entitled "A New Voyage
to Georgia," written by a young English gentleman who had visited the Cape Fear settlement, and gave his impressions of it.   It is
published in the second volume of the "Georgia
Historical Collections," and, as it describes
several interesting localities, a full extract is
here given from it.   Coming by land, with
thirteen others, along the coast from South
Carolina, this traveller says:

We left Lockwood's Folly about eight the
next morning, and by two reached the town of
Brunswick, which is the chief town in Cape
Fear, but with no more than two of the same
horses which came with us out of South Carolina.   We dined there that afternoon.   Mr.
Roger Moore, hearing we had come, was so
kind as to send fresh horses for us to come up
to his house, which we did and were kindly
received by him, he being the chief gentleman
in all Cape Fear.   His house is built of brick,
and exceedingly pleasantly situated about two
miles from the town and about half a mile
from the river, though there is a creek comes
close up to the door, between two beautiful
meadows about three miles length.   He has a
prospect of the town of Brunswick, and of
another beautiful brick house, a building about
half a mile from him, belonging to Eleazer
Allen, Esq., late Speaker to the Commons

House of Assembly, in the province of South Carolina.

There were several vessels lying before the town of Brunswick, but I shall forbear giving a description of that place; yet, on the 20th of June we left Mr. Roger Moore's, accompanied by his brother, Nathaniel Moore, Esq., to a plantation of his up the Northwest branch of Cape Fear river. The river is wonderfully pleasant, being next to Savannah, the finest on all the continent.

We reached the Forks, as they call it, that same night, where the river divides into two very beautiful branches called the Northeast and Northwest, passing by several pretty plantations on both sides. We lodged that night at one Mr. Jehu Davis's, and the next morning proceeded up the Northwest branch; when we got about two miles from thence we came to a beautiful plantation belonging to Captain Gabriel,* who is a great merchant there, where were two ships, two sloops and a brigantine loading with lumber for the West Indies: it is about twenty-two miles from the bar. When we came about four miles higher up we saw an opening on the Northwest side of us which is called Black River, on which there is a great deal of very good meadow land, but there is not any one settled on it.

The next night we came to another plantation belonging to Mr. Roger Moore, called the

---

*This name was Gabourell.

Blue Banks, where he is going to build another
very large brick house. This bluff is at least
one hundred feet high, and has a beautiful
prospect over a fine, large meadow on the opposite side of the river; the houses are all
built on the west side of the river, it being for
the most part high champaign land; the other
side is very much subject to overflow, but I
cannot learn they have lost but one crop. I
am creditably informed they have very commonly four-score bushels of corn on an acre of
their overflowed land. It very rarely overflows
but in the winter time when their crop is off.
I must confess that I saw the finest corn growing there that ever I saw in my life, as likewise wheat and hemp. We lodged there that
night at one Captain Gibbs's, adjoining to Mr.
Moore's plantation, where we met with very
good entertainment. The next morning we
left his house and proceeded up the said river
to a plantation belonging to Mr. John Davis,
where we dined.

The plantations on this river are all very
much alike as to the situation; but there are
many more improvements on some than on
others; this house is built after the Dutch
fashion, and made to front both ways on the
river, and on the land he has a beautiful avenue cut through the woods for above two miles,
which is a great addition to the house. We
left his house about two in the afternoon, and
the same evening reached Mr. Nathaniel
Moore's plantation, which is reckoned forty

miles from Brunswick.   It is likewise a very
pleasant plantation on a bluff upwards of sixty
feet high.

He then describes—after saying that he had
"not so much as seen one foot of bad land"
since leaving Brunswick—a trip he took with
Mr. Moore and others to Waccamaw Lake,
which he said he had heard so much talk of
and desired very much to see, and which, after
seeing, he pronounces "the pleasantest place
that I ever saw in my life."   The number of
deer, wild turkeys, geese and ducks greatly
astonished him, and he said they shot "sufficient to serve forty men, though there was but
six of us."   After staying a night at Newton
(now Wilmington) in a hut, and then visiting
Rocky Point, "which is the finest place in all
Cape Fear," where he was entertained by
Colonel Maurice Moore, Captain Hyrne, John
Swann, Esq., and others, he returned to Orton,
and the next day left the Province by way of
Lockwood's Folly, in regard to which place he
records a sore disappointment, as follows:

About two I arrived there with much difficulty, it being a very hot day, and myself very
faint and weak, when I called for a dram, and,
to my great sorrow, found not one drop of
rum, sugar or lime juice in the house (a pretty

place to stay all night indeed), so was obliged to make use of my own bottle of shrub, which made me resolve never to trust the country again in a long journey.

It thus appears that as early as 1734 there were comfortable and even elegant residences all along both branches of the Cape Fear for forty or fifty miles above Brunswick, and these were multiplied continually afterwards. A handsome brick building, such as this traveller found at Orton, was a great rarity at that early period, and necessarily a very costly one, as all the bricks were brought from England. It was an expensive investment in which none but rich men could possibly indulge. The status of the men who owned those on Cape Fear has been well described by one* whose unequalled knowledge of the "old times and men" of that region well qualified him for the task, and his description is here transcribed:

They were no needy adventurers, driven by necessity—no unlettered boors ill at ease in the haunts of civilization, and seeking their proper sphere amidst the barbarism of the savages. They were gentlemen of birth and education, bred in the refinements of polished society, and bringing with them ample for-

_____

*Hon. George Davis, Chapel Hill Address, 1855.

tunes, gentle manners, and cultivated minds.
Most of them united by the ties of blood, and
all by those of friendship, they came as one
household sufficient unto themselves, and
reared their family altars in love and peace.
*   *   If history immortalizes those who, with
the cannon and the bayonet, through blood
and carnage, establish a dynasty or found a
state, surely something more than mere ob-
livion is due to those who, forsaking all that
is attractive to the civilized mind, lead a colony
and plant it successfully in harmony and
peace, amid the dangers of the wilderness and
under the war-whoop of the savage.

It was long after the stranger's visit in 1734,
and after the death of these first settlers that
the events which made Brunswick famous
occurred, but the same characteristics marked
their successors, who, as long as the old town
lasted, maintained the reputation of the community for a refined and generous hospitality.

Memorable for some of the most dramatic
scenes in the early history of North Carolina
as the region around Brunswick was—being
the theatre of the first open armed resistance
to the Stamp Act on the 28th November, 1765,
and not far from the spot where the first victory of the Revolution crowned the American
arms at Moore's Creek Bridge on the 27th

February, 1776—its historic interest was perpetuated when, nearly a century afterwards, its tall pines trembled and its sand-hills shook to the thunder of the most terrific artillery fire that has ever occurred since the invention of gunpowder, when Fort Fisher was captured in 1865. Since then it has again relapsed into its former state, and the bastions and traverses and parapets of the whilom Fort Anderson are now clad in the same exuberant robe of green with which generous nature in that clime covers every neglected spot. And so the old and the new ruin stand side by side in mute attestation of the utter emptiness of all human ambition, while the Atlantic breeze sings gently amid the sighing pines, and the vines cling more closely to the old church wall, and the lizard basks himself where the sunlight falls on a forgotten grave.

APPENDIX.

The following correspondence between Governor Martin, Captain Parry and the people, at the beginning of the American Revolution, is copied from the original documents recently procured by the Secretary of State at Raleigh from England. It occurred, as the date shows, on the very day of the battle of Moore's Creek Bridge, 27th February, 1776, but probably before intelligence of that event reached Wilmington. Cornelius Harnett was almost certainly the author of the letters on behalf of the people, and the calm courage which characterizes them, displayed as it was in the face of a threat to destroy the town, will send a thrill of admiration through every generous soul who reads them:

To the Magistrates and Inhabitants
of the Town of Wilmington:

It is expected and hereby required that the Inhabitants of the Town of Wilmington do furnish for his Majestie's service One Thousand barrels of good flour on or before Saturday next, being the second day of March, which will be paid for at Market price.

JO. MARTIN.

Cruizer Sloop of War,
Off Wilmington, Feb. 27th, 1776.

CRUIZER, WILMINGTON RIVER,
Feb'y 27th, 1776.

His Majestie's ships not having received provisions agreeable to their regular Demands,

I shall, as soon as possible, be off Wilmington with his Majestie's sloop Cruizer, and other armed vessels under my command to know the reason of their not being supplied.

I expect to be supplied by six this Evening with the provisions I have now demanded of the contractor.

If his Majestie's ships or Boats are in the least annoyed it will be my duty to oppose it.

FRAN'S PARRY.

To the Magistrates and Inhabitants of Wilmington.

————

The Inhabitants of Wilmington, by their representatives in Committee, in answer to your Excellencie's demand of One Thousand Barrels of flour for his Majestie's service, beg leave to assure your Excellency that they have been always most cordially disposed to promote his Majestie's real service, which they think consistent only with the good of the whole British empire. But the inhabitants are astonished at the quantum of your Excellencie's requisition, as they cannot conceive what service his Majesty has in this part of the world for so much flour. In the most quiet and peaceable Times, when the Ports were open and Trade flourished, it would have been im-

possible to procure such a quantity in the
Town in so short a time as your Excellency
mentions. How then can your Excellency
expect a compliance from the Inhabitants of
Wilmington during the present stagnation of
Commerce? At a time, too, when you well
know that an army raised and commissioned
by your Excellency hath been for some time
possessed of Cross Creek and the adjacent
country from whence only we can expect the
Article you have thought to Demand.

We can with Truth assure your Excellency
that it is not in our power to comply with
your requisition, either in whole or in part,
many of the Inhabitants having for some time
passed wanted flour for private use, and the
dread of Military Execution by the ships of
War hath induced most of the Inhabitants to
remove their effects. The Inhabitants, Sir,
sincerely wish they had not reason to expect
that your Excellency's Demand is only a prelude to the intended destruction of the devoted
Town of Wilmington.

If this should be the case, it will not, however, make any alteration in their determination. It will be their duty to defend their
property to the utmost, and if they do not suc-
ceed altogether to their wish, they have one
consolation left, that their friends will, in a
few days, have it in their power to make ample
retribution upon those whom your Excellency
thinks proper to dignify with the epithets of
friends to Government. These faithless and

selfish people are now surrounded by three armies above four times their Number, and the Town of Cross Creek, now in our hands, will make some, tho' a very inadequate compensation for the destruction of Wilmington. This, Sir, is no boast, and we would not treat your Excellency with so much disrespect as to make use of Threats. The Acco't we have given you is sacredly true, and we have the most convincing proof of it in our possession.

I have the honor to be, by order of the Committee,

Sir, Your Excellency's most Obt Serv't.

WILMINGTON, 27th Feb'y, 1776.

Sir:

The reasons why his Majestie's ships have not been supplied with the usual quantity of provisions is so obvious that it cannot possibly have escaped the sagacity of Captain Parry. The trade of this colony hath been distressed by the King's ships, even contrary to the Acts of the British Parliament. The Military stores, the property of the People, have been seized with an avowed Intention to subjugate them to slavery, The fort which the People had built at a great Expence for the protection of their Trade made use of for a purpose the very reverse, and when they attempted to demolish it they have been fired upon by the ships of war.

The slaves of the American Inhabitants have been pursued and many of them seized and inveigled from their duty, and their live stock and other property killed and plundered, long before the Committee thought it necessary to deny the ships a supply of provisions; and to Crown all you, Sir, for the Second Time have brought up the Cruizer and several Armed Vessels to cover the landing of an army Composed of highland banditti, most of whom are as destitute of Property as they are of Principle, and none of whom you will ever see, unless as fugitives imploring protection.

Tho' you should come up before the Town you cannot expect any other answer than what we now give you.

We have not the least intention of opposing either your ships or Boats, unless you should attempt to injure us, and whenever you may think proper to treat the Inhabitants as his Majestie's officers did heretofore, we shall be happy to receive you in the manner which we always wish to receive those who have the honor to bear His Majestie's commission.

I am, by Order of the Committee,

Sir, Your Obt Servt.

To Capt. Parry.

———

To the Magistrates and Inhabitants
of the Town of Wilmington:

I have been much surprised to receive an answer to my requisition directed to The Magistrates and Inhabitants of Wilmington, from a member of the lawfull Magistracy in

the name and under the Traitorous Guize of a
Combination unknown to the laws and Constitution of this Country, as if the Magistrates
and Inhabitants of Wilmington chose rather
to appear in the Garb of Rebellion than in the
character of his Majestie's loyal and faithful
subjects.

The quantity of flour that I required for his
Majestie's service, I concluded, from the information I had received, that the Town of
Wilmington might have well supplied within
the Time I appointed by my Note, and I should
have been contented with the quantity that
was obtainable. The requisition was not made,
as the answer to it imports, for a prelude to
the destruction of that Town, which has not
been in contemplation, but was intended as a
Test of the disposition of the Inhabitants,
whose sence, I am unwilling to believe, is
known to the little arbitrary Junto (stiling
itself a Committee) which has presumed to
answer for the People in this and other In-
stances.

The revilings of Rebellion and the Gascon-
adings of Rebels are below the contempt of the
loyal and faithful People whom I have most
justly stiled Friends of Government, and the
forbearance of menaces I have little reason to
consider as a mark of Respect from the Chair-
man of a Combination founded in usurpation
and Rebellion.

JO. MARTIN.

Sir,

The Committee of Wilmington have not only been chosen by the people, but on the present occasion these very people (consisting of the freeholders) have been consulted on the propriety of their answer. That Committees are unknown to the Constitution, let those who have driven the people to that dreadfull necessity account for.

I may venture to assure your Excellency that the greater part of the People in arms against the Inhabitants of this country are, in the opinion of every gentleman and man of understanding, unworthy to be considered as respectable members of Society. That there may be some of them of a better sort embarked in a cause which, right or wrong, does them little honor, is a Circumstance for which it is easy to account.

The Inhabitants of this Town are extremely pleased to find that his Majestie's service is not in any immediate want of the flour which your Excellency thought proper to require, as it is impossible for them to comply even in part. Whoever was your Excellencie's informant that the Town of Wilmington could now, or at any other period, procure so large a quantity in so short a time, has grossly deceived you.

The conduct of the Inhabitants of this Town is well known to your Excellency, and you might have been long since assured that there did not want any new Proof of their zeal for

his Majestie's service on the one hand, or a
firm attachment to their Liberties on the other.
And whilst they are conscious of no Acts but
those which tended to assert the rights of Gᵣ
and nature, they have reason to believe t
ʰhey do not deserve the epithets of rebels aₙₒ
traitors with which your Excellency hath so
liberally loaded them.

Time alone must convince your Excellency
that the committee cannot, for any interested
purposes, descend to convey an untruth which
candor would be ashamed of.

To the Magistrates and Inhabitants of Wilmington.

As I am informed it is inconvenient to supply his Majestie's Sloop Cruizer with salt
provisions, must beg you will send a few quarters of good beef.

FRAN'S PARRY.

Cruizer, Wilmington River,
Feb'y 28th, 1776.

www.ingramcontent.com/pod-product-compliance
Lightning Source LLC
Chambersburg PA
CBHW030817020726
47499CB00006B/1962